KV-416-489

For other titles by Barbara Cartland
please see page 160

BARBARA CARTLAND

LOVE ON THE WIND

SEVERN HOUSE PUBLISHERS

This first hardcover edition published in Great Britain 1985 by
SEVERN HOUSE PUBLISHERS LTD, of
4 Brook Street, London W1Y 1AA

Copyright © Cartland Promotions 1983

British Library Cataloguing in Publication Data

Cartland, Barbara
  Love on the wind.
  I. Title
  823'.912[F]   PR6005.A765

  ISBN 0-7278-1031-6

Printed and bound in Great Britain by
Butler & Tanner Ltd, Frome and London

Author's Note

When I visited Hyderabad in February 1982 I felt spiritually moved by the Tombs of the Quth Shahi Kings and when I was ready for a plot it all fell into place from that moment.

The background and most of the people with the exception of the hero and heroine of this novel are factual. The Viceroy, Lord Ripon raised a serious conflict in India by the introduction of the Ilbert Bill. Supported in England by the Prime Minister, Mr. Gladstone, the Viceroy had no idea that the British community would openly organise themselves to almost mutinous opposition. Meetings were held in every town and 3,000 people assembled in Calcutta.

The Assam tea planters were so infuriated that they actually hatched a plot to kidnap the Viceroy. The opposition in Bengal and elsewhere became so intense that the Bill was finally drastically modified. Lord Ripon, however, was venerated and honoured by both Hindu and Muslim, while his involvement was never forgotten by the Anglo-Indians. When in 1915 his statute was erected by Indian subscriptions, no European subscribed.

Wilfrid Scawen Blunt was a British eccentric. A writer, poet, politician, naturalist, explorer, he waged political crusades to free Egypt, India and Ireland from Colonial rule. His romantic affairs were as passionate as his politics and usually frustrated.

The glorious British Residency at Hyderabad, more palatial than any Government House in India except Calcutta and New Dehli, is now a woman's College.

His exalted Highness Nizam the VIII lives in Australia. Amongst the diamonds which came from Golconda was the Koh-i-nor which graces the Crown of England.

5

Chapter One
1883

The woman moving along the deck was enveloped in the disguising robe worn by Muslims.

She moved slowly and carefully, avoiding the prostrate figures asleep who had drawn blankets over their faces so that they were unrecognisable.

Ever since the ship had left the Suez Canal for the Red Sea the weather had been hot and humid and many of the passengers in the steerage class left their overcrowded and airless quarters to sleep in the open air.

It was now two o'clock in the morning and, except for those members of the crew on the bridge or in the engine room, everybody in the ship seemed to be silent and asleep.

Moving quietly the woman reached the rail which ended at the stern and now there was only the foaming wash which poured up from the stern of the ship into waves which ruffled the surface of the smooth sea and gradually vanished away into the night.

There was a touch of phosphorus on the water and the stars overhead were reflected until it seemed as if the sky met the sea and there was no division between them.

The woman held onto the rail and looked with sightless eyes into the distance.

The British flag was hanging limp from the pole because there was no wind, and the air itself seemed heavy and almost as if that too was without life.

The woman pulled her robe a little closer round her, then taking a deep breath as if she suddenly made up her mind she clutched the rail with both hands.

Her body seemed to stiffen into an alertness as she put her foot on the bottom rail as if preparing to heave herself over.

As she did so, a quiet voice said behind her:

"I think it would be a mistake if you did that."

She gave a little cry that was almost one of terror and turned round to see the man who had spoken. He looked like an Indian, wearing a turban and dressed in the poor unidentifiable clothes of a low caste.

She stared at him and in the starlight he could see the terror in her eyes and the trembling of her lips.

"It is very foolish to do what you are contemplating," he said quietly. "Life is very precious."

"Not to . . me," the woman said involuntarily and added: "It has . . nothing to do . . with you . . please go away!"

"That is something I cannot do," he replied, "and I have no wish to play the hero and to have to rescue you."

"I do not . . want to be . . rescued."

"It is unfortunately something I should feel obliged to attempt, and you will definitely disrupt the passage of the ship and cause a commotion."

She turned her face away from him and once again hung onto the rail.

"It is my . . life," she said almost as if she spoke to herself.

"The most priceless possession anyone could have. It would be stupid to throw it away so unnecessarily."

"Unnecessarily!" she exclaimed with a sob.

Then as if she no longer had any control over herself the tears poured down her face, and her body sagged as if she was about to sink to the ground.

Without saying anything the man picked her up in his arms and carried her back the way she had come, stepping over the sleeping bodies who had not moved or taken any interest in what had been occurring.

After at first a shudder as if she would repulse him, the woman put her head on his shoulder, and he could feel the tumult of her tears shaking her whole body.

She was very slim and light, and he suspected that under her concealing robe she was wearing very little, perhaps only a nightgown.

He carried her into the bowels of the ship, along a corridor that was badly lit, then up a staircase to another deck.

Here the air seemed less oppressive, and there were more lights.

Every cabin door was firmly shut as he carried her to the end of a long corridor where there was a small Writing-Room which was empty and lit by only one light.

He put her down gently onto a chair, then as she put her hands up to her face to hide it from him the robe that had covered her head fell back. He saw that she was fair, and, as he had thought when he looked at her in the starlight, very young.

He sat down on a chair opposite her without speaking and after some seconds the girl, for she was nothing more, took her fingers from her eyes to ask:

"Why . . must you . . interfere?"

She had intended to speak angrily, but actually it was in a broken, breathless little voice.

"Suppose you tell me," the man asked, "why you should contemplate anything so wicked and wasteful?"

His choice of words surprised her, and as she took her fingers away to look up at him he thought her tear-drenched cheeks might have been those of a young child.

"I want to . . die!"

"Why so dramatically?"

"I could not think of any . . other way that was . . possible."

She spoke simply, then wiped her tears from her cheeks with the back of her fingers before she said:

"I have thought it over . . very carefully . . I cannot go on . . it is impossible!"

"Nothing is really impossible," the man said. "However dark things seem at the moment, you must not forget there is always the dawn."

"Not for . . me."

"How can you be sure of that?" he asked. "Nobody

can see into the future, and there may be when you least expect it, something very exciting and very beautiful waiting for you round the corner."

She shook her head and as she did so the robe she was wearing fell a little lower and he could see her fair hair was very long, and waved over her shoulders neatly, he thought, to her waist.

She put her hands in her lap and sat with her shoulders drooping, slumped forward in an attitude of despair.

"Why not tell me what has upset you?" he asked. "You never know, together we might find a solution."

She looked at him again as if she wondered if she could trust him.

Then as she saw his dark eyes beneath straight eyebrows, his firm mouth and square chin, she exclaimed:

"I have seen you before!"

"Where?" the question was sharp.

"At Southampton."

She was thinking as she spoke of how she had noticed him amongst the seething tumult on the Quay just before the ship had sailed.

Piles of luggage were being taken aboard at the last moment, people seeing off their friends and relations, some smiling, some in tears. There was a throng of spectators, beggars, labourers, seamen and because the ship was going East a number of soldiers!

The gangways were filled with people moving on and off the ship whose engines were always turning.

It was then she had noticed a man who looked like an Indian moving through the crowd. He seemd to be in no hurry, and at the same time there was an assurance about him that other people lacked.

He walked up the lower gangway which led to the bottom deck, and she thought as he reached it that he was the last person to step aboard before it was moved away and the ship's railing put back into place.

She had told herself he had cut it very fine and might have missed the ship altogether and yet there had been something about his carriage that told her he would not

10

make a mistake like that, but would always get what he wanted.

Now she saw as she looked at him that he was frowning, and it also struck her as strange that although he wore a turban he spoke perfect English.

She had always imagined that all Indians spoke with an unmistakable accent and a 'sing-song' note in their voices.

As if he knew what she was thinking he said after a moment:

"I will make a pact with you."

She did not answer and there was a faint smile on his lips as he continued:

"I will forget what you were intending to do tonight if I had not stopped you, if you will forget that you saw me at Southampton."

"Why should I do that?"

"Because I am quite certain that you have no wish that I should inform whoever you are travelling with that you wished to leave the ship in such an unconventional manner."

As if his words frightened her she gave a little cry and said:

"No . . of course . . not! If you tell my uncle he will be . . very angry, very angry indeed . . and he . . would . ."

She stopped and the man saw not only the terror in her face, but a red mark on her cheek which contrasted with the translucent whiteness of the rest of her skin.

Abruptly he asked:

"Who has hit you?"

She put her fingers up to her cheek and her eyes fell before his, and her lashes were dark against her skin.

For a moment she did not speak. Then she said:

"Why can you not . . understand that I . . cannot go on as I am? I cannot bear it . . any longer. Tonight he had a . . ruler in his hand and I am . . I am a coward."

The tears were back in her eyes and the man bent forward to say very quietly:

"Why do we not start at the beginning, and you tell me your name?"

He had a feeling she was about to refuse, and he said:

"It would be quite easy, if you will not tell me, for me to ask the Purser."

"No, no! You must . . not do . . that! He might tell . . Uncle Harvey."

The man opposite her stiffened.

"Are you saying that your uncle is Sir Harvey Arran?"

"You know him?" she asked. "Promise me . . promise me you will not say . . anything to him! He would be very angry . . and when he is angry . ."

She paused and the man said grimly as if he spoke to himself:

"He hits you!"

"He is . . bad tempered because he . . lived in India for . . so long. I . . I think it . . affected his liver . . and anyway he . . hates me!"

"Why should he hate you?"

"Because since Papa and Mama died I have had to live with him and I am what he calls 'an encumbrance'."

"There is no one else with whom you could live?"

"I think some of . . Papa's cousins might . . have me, but actually I think now that Uncle Harvey . . finds me . . quite useful."

"In what way?"

"I copy out the book he is writing . . and that is what . . makes him so . . angry."

"Why?"

The questions were authoritative, and she felt she had to answer them.

"His writing is . . very hard to . . decipher, and some of the words in Urdu or Hindi are difficult to . . spell. If I make a mistake he gets . . angry with me."

The man's lips tightened and after a moment he said:

"So because you are useful he is taking you with him to India."

"That is right. I have no wish to go . . anywhere with

him, but he would not let me . . stay at home when I . . begged him to let me . . do so."

There was silence. Then the man asked:

"What is your Christian name?"

"Sita."

He raised his eye-brows.

"An Indian name, and one which, as I expect you know, is that of the goddess who was proud, pure and brave."

"Then it was obviously a mistake to call me after her, as I have nothing to be . . proud about and as I have . . already told you . . I am a coward."

"Nevertheless you must try to live up to your name. You have not told me why you were given it."

"I was born in India. My father was in the Bengal Light Brigade."

"You will feel when you get there as if you have come home."

Sita stared at him. Then she said:

"I do not . . believe you!"

"It is true, and when we reach India you will know I am right. Your uncle is going to Hyderabad."

"How did you know?"

He did not answer the question but said:

"You have not yet given me your promise that if we meet again you will forget that you saw me at Southampton and here on the lower deck."

She looked at him with a puzzled expression in her eyes.

"We will meet . . again?"

"I certainly hope so, and when we do, Sita, I want to see you smiling and happy, looking like the goddess after whom you were named."

"That is . . impossible!"

"You will find you are wrong. In the meantime I want you to promise me something else."

The way he spoke sounded serious and she said a little apprehensively:

13

"What . . is that?"

"That you will never, in any circumstances, attempt to do anything so foolish and wicked as you intended to do tonight."

"Why should it be . . wicked?" I did not ask to . . come into this world . . and it is nobody's . . business if I . . choose to go . . out of it."

"I do not think your father, if he were alive, would take that view."

"Papa is dead . . but perhaps Mama who died with him . . would understand."

"I think neither of them would expect that you, having been born in India and bearing the name of one of her most admired goddesses, would try to escape from your Karma."

Sita sat up and looked at him now in a very different way.

"Why should you think that going through the miseries I suffer with Uncle Harvey is my Karma? If Papa and Mama had not been drowned when they were sailing, I should be with them now . . if I die . . I shall be with them again."

"You cannot be certain of that," the man opposite her said quietly. "What you can be certain of is that if you deliberately throw away your body, which is very valuable, you will have to be born again, and perhaps go through all the misery you are suffering now, or worse."

"What do you mean? Are you talking about reincarnation?"

"The wheel of rebirth," the man replied. "You will find it is something everyone understands in India, and is so palpably true that you will wonder how you ever doubted it could happen to you."

"I do not believe you!"

"We will have a little wager that one day you will tell me I was right."

"I have nothing with which to bet," Sita said. "Uncle Harvey gives me no money."

14

She thought as she spoke of how she had pleaded with him almost on her knees to give her a little of her own money to buy gowns with which to travel to India.

"It will be hot, Uncle Harvey," she had said to him, "and I have nothing to wear. I can hardly walk about in the heat in the clothes I am wearing now!"

"The miserable amount of money your improvident father left you when he died must be a safe-guard against your future," her uncle replied. "I am not going to live forevever, and I do not intend to leave you any of my hard-earned money."

He waited for her to make some remark and as she was silent went on:

"You will have to fend for yourself, unless somebody marries you, which is most unlikely. At least what I have put in the Bank for you will save you from starvation."

Sita had heard all this before and it always hurt her that her uncle invariably spoke of her father contemputously, as if he should have made money during his lifetime.

Her father had left his Regiment soon after he married because he could not afford it, and came back to England to try to farm a very small estate that belonged to her mother.

That he had failed had not really been his fault.

He had not enough capital to start with, he lacked experience, and the soil which had been neglected for many years was not at all productive.

Nevertheless they had been happy in the small Manor house in a little village where her father was treated respectfully as the Squire.

Because Raymond Arran was very much in love with his wife, he only occasionally regretted the Regiment and the friends he had had in India.

Somehow with very little money he had managed to enjoy life, riding in the local Point-to-Points, and training horses he bought cheaply and broke in so that he and his wife could hunt in the winter.

Occasionally they went to London to enjoy themselves

wildly and extravagantly for two weeks before they returned to try to make up what they had spent as if they had not a financial care in the world.

The Manor had been filled with laughter and love, and only when Sita found herself incarcerated as if in a tomb in the gaunt, ugly Georgian building where her uncle lived on the outskirts of London, did she know how much she had lost.

Sita somehow thought that her uncle because he had been a Judge in India, treated everybody he met as if they were criminals. That certainly was his attitude towards her.

More than this he was clearly a misogynist and had no wish to have any woman in his house and in his care.

It was only when he discovered that Sita was intelligent enough to be useful, that he condescended to speak to her at mealtimes.

Then he demanded that she should work for him, but every mistake she made infuriated him, and from first berating her angrily, he started to shake her, then hit her.

Never in her whole life had her father or mother raised a hand against her, and Sita could hardly believe it was happening.

When at first she defied her uncle he hit her harder, then when she cried it irritated him because he thought she was wasting time when she should be working.

Being in fact perceptive she began to realise that his anger was directed not only against her, but against the frustration of becoming too old for the life he had once enjoyed and the importance of his position in India.

Having lived in India for over twenty years he had few friends in England, and those he had now found him a bore.

It was therefore understandable that Sir Harvey Arran, lonely and unwanted, hated his very existence and took it out on the newest victim.

This was Sita, and she wilted before his rage like a flower without sunshine.

When the letter came asking Sir Harvey to come out to

Hyderabad, where he had been before he retired, to advise the Nizam in a very complicated legal deal, he was elated.

"I knew they could not do without me," he said. "I knew they would miss me when I had gone! There is nobody in the whole Province with my brains or my knowledge of legal affairs."

For two days he seemed younger and almost human as he decided what books he would have to take with him and his manservants began to get out his tropical clothing which had been put away since he came back to England.

It was then that Sita had asked nervously:

"Am I to . . stay here, Uncle Harvey . . while you are . . away?"

Her uncle stared at her as if it was the first time the question of what she should do had occurred to him. Then he said sharply:

"Of course, where else would you go?"

Then it suddenly struck him that because she had been working on his book and doing his letters for nearly a year, she was more useful to him than if he had to begin again with a stranger and he said:

'No, you will come with me. At least you can continue to do something to earn the amount of money I have to expend on you, week by week, month by month, and year by year."

Because she had hoped that for a little while, at any rate, she would be free of his continual fault-finding and even physical violence every time she made a mistake, Sita felt her spirits drop despairingly.

She had sometimes thought she would like to see India because her father had spoken of it in such glowing terms, and he had first met her mother when she was visiting a relative who was Governor of the North-West Province.

But Sita knew now that to go anywhere with her uncle would be like setting off for hell, and because for one optimistic moment she had thought she would be alone, the disappointment was like a physical pain.

It was a pain that seemed to intensify every day as her

uncle raged at her whenever she asked questions, and because he was on edge concerning what lay ahead he hit her even harder than usual when she made a mistake in writing his letters or copying out a manuscript.

They had sailed through a rough sea in the Bay of Biscay and although Sita had not actually been sick she felt unwell and had an incessant headache from being rocked about.

Moreover she found when they went aboard that her uncle had engaged for her one of the cheapest cabins available in the First Class.

Little more than a cupboard, and intended for a servant travelling with a First Class passenger, it was an inside cabin with no port-hole.

Every time she entered it Sita felt as if she went into her grave.

It was badly lit, but as she had no wish to sit in her uncle's cabin she was forced to write in a light that was so dim it made her eyes ache, and even though she sat up late every night, he was not satisfied when morning came that she had done enough.

Because she felt so unwell she could not eat, and when they left the Mediterranean and entered the Suez Canal, she felt so ill that she was unable to do anything but lie on her bunk.

"Do you know what you are costing me on this voyage?" her uncled had shouted at her. "Stop being lazy, and get on with your work! I want that manuscript finished by the time we reach India, and if it is not, you will be sorry!"

"I cannot .. do any more .." Uncle Harvey," Sita answered.

He had slapped her hard across the face almost knocking her down before he shouted:

"You will work, or I will beat you into it. God knows I had only one reason for bringing you with me, and for all the use you are I might as well chuck you overboard!"

It was these words that had given Sita the idea that she could save him the trouble.

She thought about it all night and the next day when her uncle had seemed more angry and more violent than usual she had known that she could bear it no longer.

She had seen from the top deck the people sleeping on deck in the stern of the ship wrapped either in a blanket or in a shapeless Muslim robe, and had known it would be a perfect disguise in which she could reach a place where she could slip into the sea without being seen.

It was unlikely that anyone in the middle of the night would be looking back the way they had come, while those on the bridge would be looking forward over the bow.

She made her plans very carefully, and ignoring the manuscript that was waiting to be copied out in her airless cabin she watched the hands of the clock until she was sure the ship would be silent and everybody asleep.

It was then she had taken the cotton cover off her bed, which was an indeterminate faded blue, and wrapped herself in it.

In her heelless slippers she moved silently from the top deck down to the second and from there down to the third without encountering anybody, and found her way to the stern.

Now she wondered why in a ship full of sleeping people there was one man who had to be awake.

Because she found herself thinking of him rather than herself she asked after a moment:

"How can you . . speak as you . . do? You may think it . . impertinent of me, but I do not . . believe you are . . Indian."

He smiled, and it made his eyes twinkle.

"If I have been inquisitive about you, Sita, I have no wish for you to be inquisitive about me."

"Why not?"

"I have my reasons. I am still waiting for your secret promise in response to mine, not to speak of me or to know me."

"And if I refuse to give it to you?" she asked with a sudden flash of spirit she had not shown before.

"In that case," he said slowly, "I will think it my duty to tell your uncle how he might have lost his niece."

Sita gave a little cry.

"How could you . . think of . . anything so . . ?" she stopped. "I think . . actually you are only . . teasing or blackmailing me."

"You can choose which you like, but what I am asking you is serious, and I think you are intuitive enough to know that is the truth."

Her eyes widened and she said:

"You are in disguise."

"I am answering no questions."

"You asked me . . a lot."

"That was different. I am doing my duty and you are trying to escape from yours."

She gave a little laugh that somehow made her seem even younger than she looked.

Then she said:

"All right, you win, but suppose I . . find I cannot . . bear it?"

"You have to give me your promise on everything you hold holy that you will not attempt anything like that again unless I give you my permission."

Sita sat up straight.

"How can you ask . . anything so . . stupid? Suppose I . . cannot find you?"

"I think we shall meet again," the man opposite her said quietly. "In fact I am sure of it."

"But I might have to . . wait until I do . . see you."

"That would be a good thing, and give you time for second thoughts."

She looked away from him and he knew that she was thinking that if what she had to suffer was completely unbearable she would not want to wait or have second thoughts.

He bent forward again and said:

"Good heavens, child! Do you not realise that the world is not only a big but a very lovely place, and what you are suffering now is only an infinitesimal part of it."

He reached out and took her hand in his.

"Shall I assure you," he asked, "that you will find happiness eventually?"

"Why . . should I? And how do you . . know?"

"Because you are young and beautiful, and you have the personality which can, if you wish to, rise above everything that frightens you. You may not believe that, but I promise you it is true."

The way he spoke made her look at him in astonishment and instinctively her fingers tightened on his as she said:

"I . . I want to . . believe you."

"Then that is half the battle. What we believe brings us what we want almost by magic because our will is a magnet although we do not always realise it."

"Is that what you . . believe?"

"It is what I learnt in a hard school, and I have never yet been disappointed."

There was silence, then Sita without taking her hand from his, said:

"You have talked of rebirth and our Karma. Does that mean you are a Buddhist?"

"I believe in all religions that are just and help man to develop himself. Faith is something which comes from our hearts, and once it is there we are no longer afraid."

"And you think . . that is what . . I will find in . . India?"

"I am sure of it!"

The way he spoke was so positive that she felt herself respond to him in a way she could not explain. Then he said:

"Now I am going to send you back to your cabin, and I promise you things will get better from this moment. Just believe and go on believing and try to be proud, beautiful and brave."

"I . . I will try," Sita said in a low voice.

Then she asked:

"How can I . . see you again? How can I find you . . just in case?"

"You will find me," he answered, "and that is another thing in which you must have faith."

He rose to his feet and lifting her hand which he still held in his he touched it to his lips.

Then almost before she was aware of it he had left the room and she was alone.

For a moment she could hardly believe that he had gone or that the whole incident had actually occurred.

Slowly she got to her feet and lifting the robe she pulled it over her head and wrapped it around her so that her face was in shadow, then went to the door.

She walked a long time before she found a stairway which led her onto the next deck, and found she was not far from her own cabin.

Everything was very quiet and only when she opened the door and saw everything was just as she had left it did she feel as if several years had passed since she had left determined to die, determined to end for ever what had become a purgatory.

She sat down on her bunk. Then suddenly she felt completely exhausted and lay down feeling she must sleep, must forget for a little while at any rate that there would be tomorrow.

Then there would be her uncle to face, and she had done none of the work he had ordered her to do that evening.

Somehow it did not seem to matter because she was thinking over what the strange man who had prevented her from drowning had said, and how she had given him her sacred promise that she would not try to kill herself again without his permission.

"How could he ask such a thing? How could I have been so foolish as to agree to what he asked?"

But all she could think of was his eyes looking into hers the darkness of them, and the way they could crinkle with amusement when she had not expected it.

Was he Indian, or was he English?

It was something she could not decide. Now when she thought of it his skin had seemed dark, darker than any

Englishman's would have been, and yet he had been curiously unforeign in the way he had spoken, and certainly in the things he had said.

"I do not understand. Why did he not go on talking to me?"

She had a sudden yearning to see him again and wondered if she went down to the lower deck whether he would be there and she could find him.

Then she knew she was being ridiculous. He had helped her and left her and everything was as it had been before.

And yet was it?

She had wanted to take her life but somehow, in some strange way, she now wanted to live, and almost as if he had drawn it for her, she could see her Karma and his meeting. Although they had gone their separate ways, they would meet again.

Was life all part of some gigantic plan thought out and laid out by some supreme Deity?

It seemed impossible, and yet to each individual person it was of supreme importance, and concerned with themselves and their Karma, wherever it should lead them.

Sita felt her eyes closing, and as she passed from reality into a dream-world she could still hear the deep voice saying:

"This is your Karma and you must be proud, beautiful and brave like the goddess after whom you are named."

*   *   *

When morning came Sita awoke to realise she had overslept and she was sure her uncle would be breakfasting in the Saloon and be furious because she was late.

And yet, strangely, she was not so afraid as she might have been.

In fact, she knew as she awoke this morning that she felt quite different. It was almost as if the sunshine was pouring into her cabin and there was spring in the air.

She dressed in a thin gown because she knew it would be very hot and went into the corridor.

There was the same moist heat there had been yesterday, and she could see the smoothness of the sea through which the ship was moving, and the cloudless sky overhead.

Regardless of the fact that she was late already she went not down to the Dining-Saloon but out onto the deck.

The horizon was hidden by a heat haze, and for the first time she felt as if she was not alone and afraid, but moving towards a new world which would be very much more exciting than the old.

Ever since she had lived with her uncle India had been very much a part of him. She supposed that was why she had hated the idea of a country which was responsible for anyone so cruel and unpleasant.

Now she remembered the way in which her father had talked of India and the beautiful pictures he had possessed which were reproductions of Rajput paintings and the drawings her mother had shown her of Palaces and elephants and gorgeously dressed Maharajahs.

She wondered what had happened to them and supposed they were in store somewhere on her uncle's property in Wimbledon where they had been taken from the Manor.

Because Sita had been so grief-stricken at losing her parents, she had not asked for anything for herself, and accepted that the only things she possessed were her clothes and those which had belonged to her mother.

Because her uncle refused to give her any money, she had been wearing those for the last two years even though many of them were too grown-up for her.

She was quite certain he would have expected her to go on doing so for ever if she had not insisted on having something new for India.

Even so, the gowns she had been able to purchase with the little money he had given her were of very cheap materials, although she had good taste and chose only what was becoming to her personally.

Vaguely at the back of her mind she remembered her mother saying that the Indian tailors could copy anything very skilfully and they would sit on a verandah stitching and making up any gown one wished with the materials one could buy in the Bazaar.

It was an attractive idea, but Sita was sure her uncle would give her no more money to spend, and if she looked a dowdy little sparrow amongst the glamorous plumage affected by other women he would not be in the least concerned.

Because in some strange manner her imagination had now suddenly been stimulated into thinking of India in a very different way from how she had before, she wished she had taken more interest in where they were going, and where they were staying.

Because her uncle had been so particularly unkind to her while they were getting ready for the voyage, and because he had been incensed with her every day since they had joined the ship, she could think of nothing but avoiding his blows.

She had wished, as she had wished a thousand times before, that she had been with her father and mother when they had drowned.

It had been just chance that they had gone out without her, for they had all gone for a summer holiday to Devonshire because her father loved sailing and he had a friend who lent him not only a tiny cottage but also his sailing-boat.

"I am afraid it is getting very old, Raymond," he said when they arrived, "and is not particularly sea-worthy. In fact I am trying to save up to buy another boat, but I dare say it will amuse you, as it has before."

"I cannot tell you how grateful I am," her father had answered, "and I hope you will enjoy yourself on the Spey and catch plenty of fish."

The reason why her father's friend, with whom he had served in India, lent him his house and his boat was that once a year he always went fishing in Scotland.

When she thought it over later, Sita was sure that he pinched and saved for eleven months of the year so that he could afford the long journey North.

In the same way her father and mother saved for the journey to Devonshire and for the case of wine they always took as a present to show their gratitude for the holiday.

Her father was like a school-boy as soon as he arrived, hurrying to the beach to look for his friend's sailing-boat, and getting it ready so that they could leave early the next morning on an expedition.

For a week they sailed almost every day along the bay, picnicking in different places below the cliffs, or sometimes eating the sandwiches and cake her mother had made, far out to sea.

On the seventh day it was raining and when Sita came down to breakfast she asked:

"Surely you will not take the boat out today, Papa?"

"I think it will be rather fun," her father replied, "but as I do not want you to get wet and catch a cold, which would be extremely unbecoming, I suggest you stay at home today."

Sita had not really minded.

She had made a friend whose family was staying in a near-by cottage, and they had promised each other when they had time to go sketching together and see who could paint the best picture of the fishermen's huts lining the bay.

"We might do that this afternoon," Sita said to herself. "If not, we will paint a picture of a vase of flowers. I know I can do that better than Jennifer."

As it happened they managed to do both, sketching the flowers in the morning and the bay in the afternoon when the rain was swept away by a strong wind.

They had to find a very sheltered spot in which they could sit and not have their drawing-paper blown away, but they managed it and only when they had been painting for a long time did Jennifer say:

"I have never seen waves as rough as this! Look! They are almost swamping those boats which are moored in the bay."

The sea was certainly very rough, but at the same time beautiful.

"I wish I could paint it!" Sita exclaimed, but Jennifer replied that it would be far too difficult and added:

"I am afraid your father and mother will have a very rough passage trying to get back to you."

It was only at midnight when Sita was distraught since they had not yet returned, that she learnt that the sailing-boat had been wrecked on the rocks about a mile from home, and both her father and mother had been drowned.

Then the world as she knew it came to an end, and when her uncle arrived to take her back to London with him, nothing was ever the same again.

Now as she stood looking over the smooth sea without even a ripple on it, Sita thought that was how perhaps her life would be in the future: smooth and no longer rough, stormy and frightening, as it had been for the last two years.

"It is too much to ask," she told herself, then heard a deep voice say:

"You must have faith!"

It was almost as if he ordered her to do what he said and she wondered as she turned and went down to the Saloon for breakfast if he was thinking of her as she was thinking of him.

Chapter Two

When Sita went down to the Saloon she found that her uncle had already eaten his breakfast and left.

She was quite certain that this would ensure that he was in a bad temper.

At the same time it was a relief to be able to eat without him glaring at her, and she enjoyed her breakfast more than she had on any other day since the voyage began.

When she had finished she walked first to her cabin to collect the manuscript that she had not worked on last night.

She then went to his cabin to find, as she expected, that he was sitting at a table he used as a desk and was waiting for her with what she thought was an ominous expression on his face.

"You are late this morning!" he said sharply as she entered. "I cannot imagine why you cannot be on time at your age, when I am extremely punctual at mine."

"Yes, I know, Uncle Harvey," she replied, "but I am afraid I overslept."

"Sleep, sleep! That is all young people think about!" Sir Harvey said irritably. "Now let us get down to work, because we have a lot to do."

Sita put the manuscript down on the desk and said:

"I am . . afraid I was . . unable to do any more last night."

"What do you mean – unable to do any more?" he asked furiously.

He snatched up the manuscript, turned it over and saw that there were no fresh pages copied out in Sita's neat, elegant writing which contrasted with his almost illegible scrawl with numerous corrections.

He stared at the pages as if he could hardly believe what he saw. Then he rose to his feet to say:

"Dammit! It is absolutely disgraceful that you have been lazing about when you should be working."

He spoke in such a furious voice that instinctively Sita moved back a few paces and felt herself begin to tremble as she always did when her uncle ranted at her.

"I . . am sorry . . Uncle Harvey," she said, "but I will . . try to . . make up for it today."

"That does not pacify me!" her uncle shouted. "Incidentally, the work you did yesterday has dozens of mistakes. Any child in a Primary School could have done it better."

He picked up the pages of Sita's writing which was lying on his desk and walked to where she was standing in the centre of the cabin to say:

"Look at this – and this! Surely you cannot be so half-witted as not to realise what this word is meant to be?"

As he spoke he held the papers in front of her and pointed out her mistakes with the finger of his other hand.

"I feed you, I keep you, when you are nothing but an impoverished orphan," he raged, "and all the thanks I get for it is sloppy, untidy work which is absolutely disgraceful!"

Because he was shouting Sita felt the tears come into her eyes. Then as he lost complete control of himself Sir Harvey thrust the papers into her hands saying:

"Correct them immediately, you stupid little fool! Then get on with the work you omitted to do last night, and if it is as bad as this, I will beat you until you do better!"

As he spoke, he raised his hand in preparation to hitting her on the back of the head, as he had done so often. As she tried to move away from him to avoid the blow, there was a knock on the door.

The sound of it made Sir Harvey's hand stay where it was in mid-air, but before he could say: "Come in!" the door opened and the Ship's Doctor entered the cabin.

He was a middle-aged man, stout, jovial and liked by all the passengers who travelled in this particular ship.

Although Sita could only see him through a haze of tears she fancied he was well aware of what was happening as he entered the cabin, and he could not have helped hearing her uncle shouting at her when he was outside.

"What do you want?" Sir Harvey asked in an uncompromising tone.

"I am sorry to disturb you, Sir Harvey," the Doctor replied, "but I was looking for your niece. I noticed she did not come down to breakfast with you, so I was worried in case she was ill."

"Ill? Why should she be ill?" Sir Harvey asked. "She was late to breakfast because she is lazy and indolent, like all young people today."

"I hope that is the only explanation," the Doctor answered, "but I want to see Miss Arran for another reason."

"What is that?" Sir Harvey asked sharply.

The Doctor shut the door behind him and coming further into the cabin said:

"It has been brought to my notice that Miss Arran might have contracted a disease which had brought out a rash on her face."

Sita stared at the doctor in astonishment.

Then she realised he was referring to the red mark where her uncle had hit her on several occasions but particularly yesterday.

She thought when she dressed that it was vividly red against the whiteness of her skin, as it had been last night, and it made her think how shocked the man who had saved her from drowning had been that her uncle should hit her.

"I . . am all . . right," she tried to say, but her voice was lost in her uncle's reply to the Doctor as he said almost violently:

"There is nothing wrong with my niece and you have no right to suggest it. She has a mark on her face, but that is not your business."

"I am sorry, Sir Harvey," the Doctor said quietly, "but it *is* my business because it is my duty to look after those who travel in this ship, and make sure that they are not suffering from anything that is contagious."

"Damned nonsense!" Sir Harvey muttered.

As if he was slightly embarrassed he sat down at his desk and started to turn over the pages of his manuscript to show he had no wish to continue the conversation.

The Doctor looked at Sita and smiled.

"I do not want to worry you unduly, Miss Arran," he said, "and I am sure you understand my position, but I must make sure these fears that have been expressed to me have no foundation in fact."

"Yes . . of course . . Dr. Johnson," Sita replied. "I quite . . understand."

"Shall we go to your cabin, or shall I just have a look at you here?" the Doctor asked.

"You will look at her here!" Sir Harvey interposed. "I have no wish for there to be any hokey-pokey going on behind my back."

"There is no hokey-pokey, I assure you," the Doctor replied, "just a very short inspection."

He smiled again at Sita and said:

"Come over to the light and let me see what is wrong with your cheek."

Sita's eyes flickered before his. She was sure that the Doctor was well aware that the mark on her cheek was caused by a blow.

She stood in front of one of the port-holes and the Doctor looked at the mark, then touched it gently with his fingers.

"Does that hurt?" he asked.

"A . . little."

"I am afraid it may turn into a rather ugly bruise, but it should not last more than a day or two."

Sita thought he had finished, but then he said:

"I hope you will not mind my asking, Miss Arran, but could I have a quick glance at your back? Infectious diseases, as I expect you know, usually start behind the ears or on the back. I would like to reassure those who are worried about you that there is nothing wrong."

As she felt there was nothing else she could say, Sita replied:

"Yes . . of course."

She turned her back to the Doctor as she spoke and put up her hands to undo the buttons of the cotton gown she was wearing.

"Let me," he said, "I am a married man, and well versed in the art of being a lady's maid!"

Sita stood still while he undid about six of the buttons at the back of her neck.

She was aware that the marks from the ruler with which her uncle had hit her last night had left red weals on her skin and when she had gone to bed she could feel them burning.

This morning her back had been stiff and hurt her as she got out of bed.

The Doctor had only made a very small opening, but it was enough for him to see the marks against the whiteness of her skin.

Then he skilfully did up her buttons again and said:

"These marks are not contagious. But listen to me, Miss Arran, and this is very important."

"I am . . listening."

"If by any chance a weal of this sort should break the skin you must come to see me at once, because in this climate it might easily turn septic."

"I understand."

"However small the open wound might be, it can be dangerous, so please attend to what I say, and do not hesitate to visit me immediately. Do you promise?"

"Yes . . of course . . Dr. Johnson. I will do as you . . tell me."

The Doctor glanced at Sir Harvey who was looking down at the papers on his desk. Then he said slowly in a manner which could not be misunderstood:

"I can only hope, Miss Arran, that there will be no need for you to suffer any further in the future."

He smiled at her in a way she felt was sympathetic and understanding and walked towards the door.

When he reached it he turned back to say in a very different tone of voice:

"Good morning, Sir Harvey!"

There was no response and the Doctor left the cabin, shutting the door quietly behind him.

When he had gone there was an uncomfortable silence which Sita was afraid to break. Then Sir Harvey said sharply:

"Come along! Get back to work! What are you waiting for! There is a great deal to do."

As he spoke Sita moved hastily towards the desk and as she reached out to pick up the papers that were lying there in an untidy heap where her uncle had thrown them, there was another knock and the door opened again.

"I forgot to say," Dr. Johnson said, "that I am moving Miss Arran into a different cabin. I saw just now where she was sleeping and I realise that it is too dark and too airless for anybody who has to work in this climate."

"I cannot afford anything more expensive," Sir Harvey thundered, "so it is no use your talking about it."

Dr. Johnson looked rather pointedly around the large, light, airy cabin in which he was standing, then said in a tone that was so pleasant that it would have been impossible for anybody to take offence:

"I have of course, Sir Harvey, taken that into consideration and there will be no extra charge. There is an outside cabin on this deck which became vacant after Port Said, and I am sure Miss Arran will find it a great deal more comfortable, and certainly more healthy."

He did not wait for a reply but shut the door again.

"That is . . very kind," Sita murmured.

At the same time her heart was singing.

She would be in a cabin from which she could look out at the sea, and she knew unmistakably that her uncle would not hit her again.

She drew in her breath at the relief of it and was certain

33

as she continued to pick up the pages in front of her who was responsible.

As if to assert his authority after what the Chinese would have called "losing face" in front of the Doctor, Sir Harvey was for the rest of the day even more disagreeable than usual.

But as he ranted and roared at her, Sita was no longer afraid as she had been in the past because she knew that physically, at any rate, he would not hurt her.

Only when she managed to escape from him by saying she would continue her work in her own cabin did she have a chance to think over what had happened, and longed to express her gratitude to the man who had saved her.

"How could he have managed it?" she asked.

And yet who else would have sent the Doctor to examine her face and be aware there were marks on her back.

It seemed incredible that a man who was travelling steerage in the bowels of the ship and was outwardly a low caste Indian could have such authority.

"I knew he was in disguise," she told herself and remembered she had given him her sacred oath not to speak of it.

All the same she wanted to thank him, and leaving the papers in her cabin she hurried up onto the top deck to look down from there into the stern thinking perhaps she would see him.

There were a number of people striving to get a breath of fresh air, sitting on the deck, most of them cross-legged in a manner that few Europeans could achieve.

Others were playing games of cards, throwing dice, or nursing children of which there were a great number.

But there was no sign of the man she wanted to see, and she stood there for a long time wondering how she could communicate with him and thinking it very foolish that while he had asked for her name, she had not asked him for his.

'Perhaps I shall see him tomorrow,' she thought.

But she had the feeling that if he did not want her to see him, it would be impossible for her to catch sight of him.

She worked in her new cabin until dinner-time, then changed into an evening-gown which had belonged to her mother, and which she was sure the other passengers would know had "seen better days".

She had managed with the meagre amount of money her uncle had allowed her to buy two new evening-gowns, but she was keeping those until she arrived in India.

She was quite certain from the way her uncle had talked of his importance in the past that they would be invited to dinner-parties.

Because Sir Harvey was so uncommunicative she had no idea where they would be staying in Hyderabad when they got there.

She had learnt since she had been living with her uncle not to ask questions because it always made him angry, and because she had been so depressed at having to go with him to India it had only seemed an extension of the misery she had known in his house in Wimbledon.

As usual Sir Harvey sat through dinner without speaking, except when he grumbled about the food.

They had been invited to sit at the Captain's table but he had refused, and Sita listened enviously to the laughter that came from his other guests.

Although they were mostly elderly people, she felt that anything would be preferable to sitting alone with her uncle and not daring to open her mouth in case she said something wrong.

When dinner was finished he said:

"You had better get back to work, and see that what I have given you is finished before breakfast-time tomorrow morning."

"I will do . . what I can . . Uncle Harvey, but I . . doubt if I shall be able to . . finish it all."

Because they were in a public place Sir Harvey had to bite back the furious words he would have used if they had been alone, and instead walked away into the Smoking Room, as if he was as glad to be rid of her as she was of him.

Sita hesitated for a moment. Then she went out on deck.

There were quite a number of people either walking slowly in the hot and moist air or standing at the railings, looking at the phosphorous on the water.

Because she felt shy at being alone she climbed up onto the deck above where there was only the lifeboats and where few people ventured during the day because there was no awning over their heads.

As she expected, there were only a few couples sitting very close together, their arms around each other.

Avoiding them, Sita went to the isolated seat where she had been before.

She sat down and looked up at the stars overhead, thinking how beautiful they were and at the same time how insignificant they made human beings seem.

She must have sat there for nearly an hour thinking of herself and what the man who had rescued her the night before had said about the wheel of rebirth.

"Is it possible I have really lived in this world previously?" she asked herself. "If so I must have behaved very badly, and now I am being punished for my sins by having to live with Uncle Harvey!"

It was difficult to contemplate, and yet at the same time, when she thought of it, it seemed a terrible waste that one should live and suffer and perhaps rise by drive and persistence above any circumstances however adverse and then end in nothing but a grave in a Church-yard.

Alternatively if the Christian teaching was to be believed one was swept into a vaguely defined Paradise which would be certainly very overcrowded with all the people who had lived on earth for thousands and thousands of years.

"It is too . . difficult to . . understand," she said aloud.

"What is?" a voice asked beside her.

36

She started, but even as she did so she knew this was what she had been waiting and hoping for.

He was there, and she was so pleased to see him that she forgot it might be unconventional to be too effusive.

"You are here! I have been thinking of you and wanting to see you all day," she said. "I looked but I could not see you."

She could not be sure, but in the starlight she thought he smiled.

Then as she looked at him she thought he looked different, then realised it was because he was not wearing a turban.

"How are you?" he asked.

"You sent the Doctor to see me," she said, "and I have to . . thank you for . . changing my cabin."

"I think you are supposing a lot of things which I do not admit.

"You are the . . only person who could have helped me," Sita said simply, "and I am very . . very grateful."

Her eyes were watching his face as she spoke, though it was very hard to see clearly in the light from the stars.

Yet she felt somehow her instinct was more important than her eyes, and she knew he was looking at her kindly, and was trying to help her as he had helped her before.

Then she asked:

"How did you . . find me? How did you . . know I was . . here?"

"I knew it was likely that you would want to be outside on such a wonderful night, and you would be too shy to move about in the crowd on the deck below."

"That is true, but I am . . surprised you . . realised it."

"Shall I say that I was trying to think as you would think."

"Is that a . . difficult thing to . . do?"

She clasped her hands together. Then she said:

"You are very mysterious . . and yet it is exciting for me to meet . . somebody like you . . apart from the fact that you have now . . saved me twice . . once from drowning . . and now from . . my Uncle."

"I do not think he will hurt you any more."

Again she thought the man beside her smiled before he added:

"Forget all that for the moment. I want to make sure that you are happier than you were last night, and also looking forward to what lies ahead."

"I had not really thought about it until now," Sita said, "but I have been trying to remember all the things Papa said about India, which he loved, and I will try to love it too."

"That is what I wanted you to say, and I shall be very disappointed if you do not find it not only enjoyable, but a spiritual experience which you have never known before."

"Will I see . . you there?"

"I am sure we shall meet."

"Where . . and how?"

"I think we must leave that to our Karma. When you begin to understand you will find that nothing happens by chance or coincidence, but there is a definite pattern in everything we do and everything that happens."

Sita thought for a moment. Then she said:

"That is reassuring."

"That is what I want you to feel."

"Why?"

"Because then you will not be afraid, and you will know that you are developing yourself hour by hour, day by day."

He paused before he went on:

"Have you ever seen a little cascade running down the side of a mountain? A little silver streak which when it reaches the bottom becomes a stream which grows and widens until it reaches the river, and the river moves on slowly, but relentlessly, until it reaches the sea."

Sita gave a deep sigh.

"I understand what you are saying, but at the moment I do not feel like a cascade! Only perhaps like one tiny drop of water which will . . trickle into it by . . mistake."

The man beside her laughed. Then he said:

"I think you underrate yourself, but as long as a tiny drop moves forward and onwards it will eventually reach the sea."

There was silence, and he added:

"Of course, you will have many adventures on the way, and that is what makes life so exciting."

Because she wanted to argue with him Sita said:

"But for some people it is . . frightening . . agonising . . an abject misery."

"Such things are inevitable, but just as we have our bad times, we also have our good ones, and like the waves of the sea if they go down they are bound to come up! The only thing that matters is your faith and belief that it will happen."

"Now we are back to faith again," Sita said, "and if you have no faith . . what then?"

"You will find it, or rather it is there within yourself waiting to be discovered."

Sita looked up at the stars and said:

"Before you joined me I was . . thinking of how . . totally insignificant . . I am."

"And now?"

"Now in some . . strange way you are making me . . feel that I have a . . definite importance in the world . . if it is only to . . reach the . . sea!"

"Everybody is important," he replied, "and only at the end of your life will you look back and realise how many people have been influenced, helped and changed by you! Even now the events in your life, although perhaps you had no idea of it at the time, can alter history."

Sita laughed and it was a truly joyous little sound.

"Now you are making me feel," she said, "as if I shall suddenly be crowned Queen, or become another Joan of Arc saving France from her enemies."

"Why not? More unlikely things have happened."

"This as far as I am . . concerned is very . . very . . unlikely, but after what you have said . . I shall start . . hoping!"

"Do that," he said, "and you may find eventually that you surprise yourself."

"I think really I want to surprise you," Sita replied, "so please tell me where I can find you . . and before you . . leave me . . tell me your . . name."

She looked at him pleadingly as she spoke, but he shook his head.

"No," he said, "you have given me your sacred word of honour that you will never mention to anybody that we have met or that you have ever seen me. When we do meet again, I shall be a stranger to whom you will be formally introduced."

"But I want to . . think about you . . now."

"I have an idea you will do that anyway, just as I shall think of you."

"I want you to do that," Sita said simply, "but I also want to be sure that you are there . . . that you can save me . . perhaps for a third time . . as you have saved me . . twice already."

"Then you have to believe that our Karmas are joined, and when the moment of necessity arises I shall save you."

"And in the . . meantime?"

"In the meantime I have broken all my own rules by coming and talking to you again. But shall I say I had to see if you were happier and things were better, as I intended them to be?"

"Of course they are better . . and I am very . . very . . grateful. I want to thank you . . and go on thanking you . . but I am . . afraid of . . losing you."

She was quite certain this time that he was smiling as he replied:

"I do not think that either of us will lose each other. Goodnight, Sita, and take care of yourself."

He lifted her hand to his lips as he had the night before and she felt their touch on her skin.

Then, as it gave her a very strange feeling almost as if a shaft of moonlight moved within her body, he was gone.

Silently he had vanished in the same manner as he had

appeared and she felt she had dreamt his presence beside her and the strange conversation that had taken place.

Then as she looked up at the stars she knew that he had given her what he had told her to seek – faith in the future.

* * *

The following night, after a long day of working at her uncle's manuscript until her head ached, Sita went again to the top deck.

Although she sat there under the stars for nearly two hours he did not come, and she was alone.

It was a disappointment which was almost like a physical pain, but when she went to the small but comfortable cabin which was now hers, she was sure that he was thinking of her as she was thinking of him.

"Why did he not come and see me?" she asked.

She wondered as she had wondered a dozen times already why he was travelling as he was.

She had the feeling that it was not because he was poor, and that if he was disguised it must have been of importance that he should be.

Vaguely at the back of her mind she remembered her father telling her years ago that there was an organisation in India called '*The Great Game*'.

"It was a kind of Secret Service," he said, "and those who are in it endure danger, suffering and often death simply because they love India."

"But who is the enemy, Papa?"

"At the moment the Russians," her father replied, "who are doing their best to inflame the tribesmen on the North-West Frontier. They supply them with arms and teach them how to ambush our soldiers and cause endless trouble which inevitably leads to loss of life."

"But why should they do that?"

"Because they themselves would like to conquer India, and they are also jealous of our position in the world and wish to make everything as difficult for us as possible."

Her father had been silent for a moment. Then he had gone on as if he thought it out for himself:

"They infiltrate everywhere, turning caste against caste, Hindu against Muslim, and it is difficult to detect or stop them before trouble actually erupts in different parts of the country."

"Were you ever in '*The Great Game*', Papa?"

Her father had shaken his head.

"Not directly. Of course we all helped when we could but the chaps who actually do the work are extremely intelligent, and it was very difficult to detect who they were, unless they were actually involved in a situation in which they needed the help of troops."

Sita was intrigued and asked him to tell her more, but she soon realised her father did not know very much that he could tell her, except that those who were in '*The Great Game*' were anonymous and known only by numbers.

"Are only Englishmen members?" she enquired.

"Good heavens, no!" her father replied. "There are Indians of every sort who help because they know that the Russians are trouble-makers, and to be conquered by them would be very much worse than to be ruled by us."

"Are there any books written about '*The Great Game*'?" Sita enquired, thinking she would like to read about it.

"If there are, I do not know of them," her father replied. "It is something that is best not talked about in case inadvertently one of our members is detected, and loses his life in consequence."

Sita had almost forgotten this conversation until now.

When she thought about it, she was sure that her friend who had saved her from drowning, was in '*The Great Game*'.

Although it seemed incredible, he had changed her whole outlook in the short while they had talked together.

"There is so much I want to learn," she told herself, but was sure if he was beside her he would say that India would teach her.

Although Sir Harvey was extremely disagreeable for the next few days Sita knew it was doubtless due to the fact that he was looking forward to being back in the country where he had worked for so long, but was also apprehensive in case he was not as welcome as he hoped to be when he arrived there.

She eventually learned, although it was not from him, that the ship was going to Calcutta, which was the seat of the British Raj and where the Viceroy reigned supreme.

Since the days of the East India Company, and when the Indian Mutiny had made it imperative for the Government to take over, India had become the most valuable property of the English Crown.

The Viceroy knew that his was a unique and Imperial trust, and protecting India was one of the prime purposes of British Foreign Policy.

When the ship docked in Calcutta Sita was not sure what she expected, but it was certainly not what she saw or what happened.

To begin with, the moment they docked a resplendent *Aide-de-Camp* appeared to inform Sir Harvey that he was to be the guest of the Viceroy before he moved from Calcutta to Hyderabad.

Sita was aware from the expression on her uncle's face and the manner in which he responded, how gratified he was at such recognition.

When they drove away from the ship in an open carriage with out-riders on either side of them, and the Aide-de-Camp sitting on the seat opposite to them, she could hardly believe it was happening.

The streets were narrow, and never had she imagined there could be so many people packed in one area, or that they could be so colourful.

At the same time she realised that many sitting, eating, washing and sleeping on the pavements were in rags, naked and impoverished.

The contrast to the resplendence of their carriage and the red and white uniforms of the servants was so extreme that she found it hard not to be critical.

They reached the enormous and imposing house which the *Aide-de-Camp* told her had been built by the Marquis of Wellesley, a century earlier, as he considered the existing Government House at that time was not befitting to his position.

"It was finished in four years," the *Aide-de-Camp* explained, "and is the finest Government House in the world."

Sita looked suitably impressed, but when she actually saw the House she felt she was gaping at it like a village yokel with her mouth open.

Flanked by a pair of arched gateways crowned with lions, the huge centre block with its four wings joined by curving corridors made it seem impossible that it would house only one family.

Because it was so large her eyes were bewildered by a grandeur she had never envisaged in her whole life.

The Marble Hall adorned with canvasses of gods and goddesses, the furnishings, the mirrors which came from the Palace of the deposed Burmese King, the Louis XV chairs and settees in the State Drawing-Room made her feel that she must look at them and go on looking so that she would never forget how magnificent they were.

She had been taken on her arrival to the Guest Wing which was reached by walking through the Marble Hall with its huge round pillars, and found that in their apartments they were waited on by what seemed to Sita to be a dozen different servants.

"They have certainly not forgotten me, even if I have not been in India for two years!" Sir Harvey said in a tone of satisfaction.

In fact he was so pleased by his reception he seemed for once to be quite human.

Only after she had had the excitement of dining with the Viceroy and Vicereine and with their personal guests, who numbered forty, did Sita realise astutely that there was another reason for her uncle having been invited to be the guest of the Viceroy besides what he believed was his own importance.

Because she was clever enough to put two and two together she learnt from what her partner said to her at dinner and from one of the remarks her uncle made later that the Viceroy, the Marquess of Ripon, was in fact 'picking his brains'.

What it amounted to was that Lord Ripon was preparing to introduce a Reform, called the 'Ilbert Bill' which would give Indian judges the right to try Europeans.

Although she knew very little about India, from the way people spoke Sita realised this was so revolutionary that almost the entire European population of India were opposed to such a measure.

The Viceroy in consequence was anxious to gain the support and expertise of Sir Harvey before he went on to Hyderabad.

As far as Sita was concerned, whatever the reason for bringing them to Government House, it was so exciting and overwhelming to be there that she knew it was something she would never forget.

The floors were of black stone, polished and shining like a mirror, so that she was almost afraid to walk on them.

Before she went to bed one of the *Aides-de-Camp* took her to the Great Hall to see the Throne on which the Viceroy sat as representative of the Queen. She thought it was perfectly beautiful, supported by four pillars of gold with hangings of crimson enriched with a golden fringe.

Nevertheless she was told that actually the house was terribly inconvenient. The kitchen was not even just outside the house, but actually outside the grounds in a narrow squalid street.

As one of the previous Vicereines had said:

"The kitchen is somewhere in Calcutta, but not in this house."

It seemed incredible that the food had to be carried across the garden two hundred yards in wooden boxes on men's shoulders.

When they arrived she asked for a bath and was appalled when she learnt that one man heated the water, another fetched the bath, a third filled it, and a fourth emptied it.

When she asked the reason she was told:

"Each man belongs to a different caste."

After all this commotion it was difficult to dress in the light of several smoking candles.

She wondered why Lord Ripon did not do something to alleviate such inconvenience, but thought perhaps he was too busy.

In the Drawing Room everyone gathered before the Viceroy and Vicereine appeared. Then the men bowed and the ladies curtsied.

At dinner there was a footman in his white and red uniform emblazoned with the Royal insignia behind every chair.

From her neighbours at dinner Sita learnt that in the garden there were flying foxes in every tree and night jackals which howled in the shrubberies.

"What is more," her informant continued, "Civet cats climb into the eaves and sometimes enter the bedroom windows. My wife once found one five foot long drinking a glass of milk at her bedside!"

Here again were extraordinary contrasts. India seemed full of them.

Before they left Calcutta Sita saw the Viceroy leave Government House, and that, more than anything else, made her aware of his importance.

He was driving in an open carriage with postillions and a mounted escort of 130 bodyguards.

The magnificent troopers, tall as Lifeguards in their scarlet and gold jackets, high boots and zebra-striped *puggarees*, also mounted guard on the stairs and in the corridors.

All the upper servants at Government House were dressed in scarlet and gold, and Sita finally decided that it was more like a Palace in 'The Arabian Nights' than anything she had ever dreamt about.

At the same time she was so afraid of doing anything wrong that it was quite a relief when they were escorted as they had been on arrival to the Railway Station where they were to take the train to Hyderabad.

Then because Lord Ripon was so anxious for her uncle's support, Sita discovered that they had been given the Viceregal coach to be attached to the train.

Painted white and gold, it was certainly more impressive than the ordinary carriages, and they were treated with almost reverent respect by those serving the railway.

The *Aides-de-Camp* who saw them off stood at the salute as the train steamed out of the station, and only when they were alone did Sita say to her uncle:

"I only wish, Uncle Harvey, that people in England could see how distinguished you are in India."

There was a faint smile on his thin lips as he replied drily:

"I doubt if they would believe it, and I only hope our reception in Hyderabad is the same as we received here."

"I hope so too," Sita said. "We might almost have left England for another planet!"

She thought as she spoke that it was exactly like a dream or rather being swept into a fairy-tale land.

Then she told herself there was only one thing missing, and that was the 'Prince Charming' who would make her story complete.

Because he was never far from her thoughts, she was thinking of the man who had saved her on the ship, and wishing that she could talk to him and that he could explain to her about India and answer all the questions that kept coming to her mind.

Then she knew, just as she could not help seeing the poverty and the squalor in the over-crowded streets of Calcutta, that was one part of India, and the Viceroy's House was another.

There was also another India, she had yet to discover!

The India of which he had spoken, the India of rebirth, and their Karma which would join them together because it was part of a design over which they as individuals had no control.

Chapter Three

By the time they reached Hyderabad, Sita had with some difficulty, because it was hard to extract any information from her uncle, learnt that it was the Capital of the Nizam's dominion, and the largest and therefore the most important Province in the whole country.

It was situated amongst trees and artificial lakes, surrounded by bare granite hills and weirdly shaped rocks which looked as if they had been thrown about by giants, and Sita noticed that the crowds in the streets were different from those in Calcutta.

Because Hyderabad was the last surviving fragment of the Mogul Empire there were people in Arab dress, descendants of the Chieftains, and soldiers from Muscat and Hadramunt and, as somebody was to explain to her later, a prevailing atmosphere which was not so much Arabian or Southern Indian as Persian.

The Nizam had maintained the independence of his vast Kingdom by entering into Treaties of friendship with the British.

The British Resident in Hyderabad therefore was not, Sir Harvey told her somewhat reluctantly, an agent of a conquering power, but more like the Ambassador of an ally.

He however wielded very great authority as the actual Ruler of certain territories ceded by the Nizam, and he controlled a number of British troops stationed immediately north of the capital and officially intended for the Nizam's use.

This all sounded somewhat bewildering, and yet when Sita saw the Residency she was prepared to believe that the Resident, Mr. John Graham Cordery, a stout and red-faced man, was very important indeed.

The Hyderabad Residency was very, very large and extremely grand, and even more breath-taking than the Governor's house in Calcutta.

She found herself gaping once again when she saw a flight of twenty-two marble steps with a colossal Sphinx on each side leading up to a portico of six dazzlingly white Corinthian columns, a Durbar hall lined with Ionic columns, and a magnificent staircase dividing into two gracefully curving flights that seemed planned for grandioise entertainment.

What however was to Sita much more interesting than anything was that the first night at dinner her partner Mr. Barnes, who was the First Secretary in the Residency, told her why this enormous house had been built.

"It would not have happened," he said, "if the Resident Major James Achilles Kirkpatrick, who came here in 1797 had not had two great loves in his life."

Sita looked at him with interest as he went on:

"The first was Kirkpatrick's love of splendour. He found the old Residency uncomfortable and inconvenient. He therefore planned immediately to built a house which he thought would be worthy of his position as the most important Resident in the Political Department."

"He certainly succeeded."

"Only by being clever," the First Secretary answered.

Sita waited and he explained:

"Before he could build the house he had to obtain a grant from the Nizam of 60 acres on the opposite side of the Musi River to the city."

"That is where we are now?" Sita asked.

Mr. Barnes nodded.

"When Major Kirkpatrick showed the Nizam a large scale plan of the proposed Residency, his request was turned down."

"Why was that?"

"The Nizam's Minister explained that he had been frightened by the size of the actual plan."

"So what happened?"

"Major Kirkpatrick was clever enough to have the same

plan drawn on a tiny card and when he again presented it to the Nizam he immediately obtained a grant!"

Sita laughed.

"That was very clever of him!"

"It has unfortunately not been reported what the Nizam said when he saw the finished project," Mr Barnes smiled, "and you have not asked me what was Major Kirkpatrick's second love."

"What was it?"

"The Resident fell in love with a beautiful Muslim girl called Khair-un-Nissa."

Sita listened wide-eyed and he went on:

"Khair-un-Nissa's name means Excellent among women, and the Resident, who was extremely handsome and had a gallant career, was known as 'Hushmat Yung' or Glorious in Battle."

"But surely," Sita asked, "the ladies of the Nizam's family were in purdah?"

"Of course," Mr. Barnes answered, "but the story is that Khair-un-Nissa, who was the daughter of a Persian nobleman saw Major Kirkpatrick by chance and fell in love with him."

"What happened?"

"She was brave enough, or one might almost say reckless enough to enter his house when he was alone one evening. She told him she was desperately in love and that as her Karma was linked with his, she would be content to spend the rest of her days with him as the humblest of hand-maidens."

Mr. Barnes laughed.

"As she was very beautiful, it was not surprising that Major Kirkpatrick was intrigued."

"So what did he do?"

"Khair-un-Nissa said she was being forced into marriage with a cousin but would rather end her life by poison than become his wife."

"She must have loved Major Kirkpatrick very much," Sita said beneath her breath.

"Her love was certainly ardent enough to make Major

Kirkpatrick, who was a very chivalrous man, tell his brother: 'I must have been something more or less than a man to hold out any longer'."

"So what happened?"

There was a hesitation as if Mr. Barnes thought the story not quite suitable for a young girl before he said in a somewhat repressed tone:

"After a son had been born the Major decided to make Khair-un-Nissa his lawful wife, and built her a house in the Residency grounds."

"Was that possible?" Sita asked.

She remembered that her father had said that any relationship between an Englishman and an Indian woman of rank was strictly forbidden by the East India Company for fear he would fall under the influence of her family.

"The Nizam forestalled any opposition from some of his family," Mr. Barnes answered, "by making Major Kirkpatrick his adopted son."

"What did the English say?"

Mr. Barnes smiled.

"The Resident was in trouble with the East India Company, and with the Governor-General who was then the Marquess of Wellesley and ordered an enquiry."

"That must have been frightening."

"Major Kirkpatrick was too clever for him. The future Governor of Bombay who was to conduct the Enquiry in Hyderabad was met by the Commandant of the Resident's personal escort. He managed to convince the future Governor, who was a sensible Scot, that if he appeared in the Nizam's Capital, it would lower the Resident's prestige even if the charges against him were proved false."

"What happened?" Sita asked.

"He returned to Calcutta, and eventually Major Kirkpatrick was able to justify himself to the Marquess."

"It is a thrilling story," she exclaimed, "and did they live happily ever after?"

"By all accounts they were very happy," Mr. Barnes replied, "and Major Kirkpatrick built a *Zénana* for his wife."

51

"Is it still here? Can I see it?"

"Yes, of course. It is decorated with paintings of birds and flowers. It has fountains to cool the air and is surrounded by an enclosed garden. It is known as the Begum's garden, but although the Resident's staff would see him walking in the direction of the *Zenana* they never set eyes on his wife who lived in strict *purdah* not even coming out to admire the new Residency when it was finished."

"How sad! She must have longed to see it."

"Her husband had a model of it built in her garden so that she could see what it was like. As you can imagine, it became a delightful playground for future generations of Resident's children. But it gradually became the haunt of snakes and so it is a mistake now to enter what is left of it."

Sita clasped her hands together.

"It is a lovely story, and I have a feeling that both Major Kirkpatrick and his Persian lady were very happy together."

She thought as she spoke of the man she had met on the ship.

If he were an Indian she wondered if in the same position, she would have dared to approach him, it being strictly forbidden for her to do so; or whether he would be brave enough to marry her when he knew it would offend his superiors.

Then she was surprised and shocked at her own thoughts.

Yet because of what Mr. Barnes had told her, she was even more interested in the enormous, beautiful house than she had been before.

The staircase, adorned with sculptures of gods and goddesses – Apollo, Venus, Leda and the Swan – all seemed part of a love-story.

Even the furniture which had come from Carlton House in London, and which the Directors of the East India Company had bought from the Prince Regent and made the Nizam pay for, had a magic all of its own.

She was to learn more of the Residency's history up to the present day, and she learned too that the Nizam when he visited the Resident, arrived on an elephant with two others as an escort.

When she was told this Sita clapped her hands together and said:

"I do hope I shall see him and the elephants while I am here."

At her enthusiasm Mr. Barnes laughed again.

"It is very likely," he said, "for the present Nizam, who has been a minor until now, is about to be installed on his throne by the Viceroy."

"You mean he is coming here?" Sita gasped.

Mr. Barnes nodded.

"I think you will be impressed by the pageantry and ceremony."

Sita was so excited that she could not hide her enthusiasm from her uncle.

"There will be processions, elephants and fireworks!" she said. "It is so fortunate we are here, Uncle Harvey!"

"That is what the Viceroy feels," Sir Harvey said complacently, "for he intends to renew the talks he had with me in Calcutta."

There was a gratified note in his voice that Sita did not miss, and she said quickly:

"I am sure it is very lucky that you should have come to India just at the right time to be able to help him."

"It certainly seems fortunate," Sir Harvey agreed.

Sita wondered if it had been his Karma.

She had found since their arrival in India that her uncle was far more pleasant to her than he had ever been before, and she knew it was because he was happy.

"It is unhappiness," she reasoned, "that makes people cross and disagreeable, so what everybody should strive for is happiness so that they can give love and understanding to everyone around them.

It was something she thought about when she was alone, and as she wandered round the huge building she was sure that the love which had made Major Kirkpatrick build it in the first place, and the love he had found with his Persian wife, had left an atmosphere which even a hundred years of other Residents had not completely obliterated.

She found at the Residency that among the other guests besides her uncle and herself, were the poet and writer Wilfrid Scawen Blunt and his wife Lady Anne, who was Lord Byron's grand-daughter.

She was very rich, while Blunt although handsome and well-born, was almost penniless.

Always impetuous, he was violently supporting the idea of home rule for all nations under the domination of the British.

He had already tried to interfere in the political situation in Egypt, and failed. Now he was anxious to try in India.

Tipoo Sahib's grandson was disappointingly cautious, and being a Government Official a Muslim Judge was afraid to be seen talking to him.

When the Blunts reached the Residency in Hyderabad, Wilfred boldly informed them:

"I favour the abolition of the entire Indian civil Service!"

Behind his back, the Resident laughed saying:

"At least he is an open enemy!"

Blunt soon realised Sir Harvey's importance in legal matters, learnt that he had stayed at Government House in Calcutta and had been consulted by the Viceroy concerning his Reform Bill.

He had already heard when he was in Calcutta that the auguries were not favourable and Anglo-Indian pressure was doing everything possible to emasculate it.

"I cannot understand anyone paying a moment's attention to Anglo-Indians!" Sita heard Wilfrid Blunt say aggressively.

The silence in which this statement was received by other people staying in the house and by the First Secretary to the Resident told her clearly what their feelings were.

Things were made worse when it was learnt that in reply to an optimistic Indian newspaper editor who suggested that Indians might be allowed to enter the Civil Service Blunt had said:

"Nothing will be done without a Revolution!"

Because Sita was not certain what to think and it was all so new to her, she found herself longing to be able to talk over such matters with her friend from the ship.

'He would understand,' she thought.

She felt that if, as she suspected, he was playing the part of an Indian, he would know what was best for India, and that was surely what everybody who loved the country would want.

There was however a great coolness the third night at dinner, and Sita, who was always sensitive to atmosphere, realised that a number of the guests, all very distinguished, were sending Wildrid Scawen Blunt who was talking more dramatically than usual to 'Coventry'.

"What has happened?" she asked Mr. Barnes who she found was the one person in the Residency always ready to answer her questions.

"I am afraid our poet is in disgrace."

"What has he done?"

"He had a meeting with some of the Muslims today in the city, and told them that all nations were fit for self-government, but few more so than the Indians."

Sita did not need Mr. Barnes or anybody else to tell her that this sort of attitude would certainly not be popular with the English, even though the Viceroy was prepared, despite a great deal of opposition, to try to give the Indian Judges extended legal rights.

One thing that delighted her was that her uncle was so busy having meetings with the representatives of the Nizam who had originally asked him to come to Hyderabad, that he had little time either to talk to her or to give her instructions.

This meant that she could enjoy herself exploring the city which was even more fascinating than she had thought it to be at first.

She enjoyed the comfort of the carriage driven by the Resident's uniformed servants, escorted by an *Aide-de-Camp* and protected by two outriders.

It was amusing to see the crowds somehow clear a way to the narrow roads to let them pass and when Sita waved to them they waved back with what she liked to think was affection as well as interest.

She learned however there were a great many places of interest outside the city which were more easily reached on horse-back than by any other means of transport.

Somewhat tentatively she asked Mr. Barnes if it would be possible for her to ride and when he told her that it could easily be arranged she was so afraid that her uncle would somehow prevent it that she did not tell him what she was doing.

"I think it would interest you," Mr. Barnes said, "and I wish I could take you myself, to see the tombs of the Quth Shahi Kings. The view from there is wonderful."

"I would love to see them."

"Very well, I will arrange it," Mr. Barnes promised. "I will send two escorts with you, one an elderly man who will take care of you, and who speaks quite good English. You had better leave early in the day before it gets hot."

Sita was so excited that it was difficult for her to sleep. She was up before she was called and dressed herself quickly in the thin riding-habit she had been wise enough to bring with her.

To pay for it meant she had to sacrifice one of the gowns she really needed.

But her habit that she had worn before her parents' death was not only too tight for her but was of a thick material which might be sensible in England, but would be intolerably hot in India.

She therefore managed to find a dressmaker who made her a wide skirt of blue piqué and a little jacket trimmed with white braid.

It was not particularly well made, but she knew that as the piqué was the same colour as her eyes, it was very becoming.

She thought that when it gew hot later in the morning she could take off her jacket and just ride in the thin muslin blouse that she had managed to buy cheaply in a sale.

She had been quite right in thinking she would look like a little sparrow amongst the elegant and beautifully gowned ladies who were the Resident's other guests.

Lady Anne appeared night after night in a different evening-gown, all so resplendent that Sita knew it was no use even beginning to try to compete with her.

Because her own gowns had been cheap, the bustle was not very large and the drapings in the front, as demanded by fashion, not particularly well arranged.

But at least because she had chosen them with care they showed off the smallness of her waist and the soft curves of her figure.

What could not be bought in a shop was the whiteness of her skin and the excitement in her eyes that made them shine brighter than any diamonds.

Because she had no other adornment she asked a little nervously if she could have some flowers, and every night the servants who waited on her brought her orchids in different colours, hibiscus flowers, and sprays of brilliant blossom from the trees that encircled the Residency.

Sita did not know if anybody else was impressed, but she herself felt before she went downstairs to the Drawing Room where they were waiting before dinner, that she at least would not look crushed or absolutely insignificant.

Because she was enjoying herself she bore no resemblance at all to the frightened girl who had found the grey house in Wimbledon a prison and her uncle a very unpleasant gaoler.

'I am free, at least for the moment,' she thought.

It was not only the influence of her new surroundings but the fact that the man who had talked to her on the ship had raised her eyes to the stars and she was no longer afraid of life or had any wish to die.

When she had breakfasted alone because it was too early for her uncle, for which she was very thankful, she left a message for him that she had gone riding and hurried to where the horses and her escort were waiting.

Because she had ridden all her adult life with her father, Sita was a good rider and had learned how to control the most obstreperous and untamed horse.

The one she was given now was an exceptionally fine animal and she was aware he needed exercise. At the same time he was well broken in and not upset at having a woman rather than a man in the saddle.

They set off, and were soon outside the city, moving west alongside the wide Musi River.

Then passing the Barracks of the Siddi Risala, the African Cavalry Regiment of the Nizam, they came to the wild land where there were huge bare, grey boulders unlike anything Sita had ever seen before.

They rode on keeping where possible to a dusty track, although sometimes stones and boulders made it impossible for them to do so.

The older man as Mr. Barnes had said, spoke a little English, and he pointed out in the distance the Golconda Fort, the perimeter of which Sita had heard was seven miles round. She had made up her mind she would visit it if she had the chance.

The great Fort had been the capital of the Quth Shahi potentates which had dazzled the eyes of Marco Polo besides the great Emperors Akbah and Shah Jehan.

"The Fort is impregnable, Lady Sahib," Sita's escort said, "only captured once by treachery."

She smiled at the pride in his voice before she replied: "Another day you must show it to me."

A mile further on they came to the Tombs, and as they rode through a grey stone gateway in a large garden Sita saw the domes of the Tombs silhouetted against the sky and thought they were very beautiful.

Because she had no wish to have anybody talking to her or walking with her while she inspected them, as she dismounted she told the two men to stay where they were, and they took her horse and theirs under the shade of a large tree in blossom.

Sita walked up the steps of the first Tomb and saw it was a square building with a huge dome on a base or chabutra and inside a gallery with pointed arches.

She did not quite know why, but immediately she saw the seven domes and the lotus friezes of leaves and buds which ornamented the outside of each small building she felt as if she was drawn to them by her heart rather than by her eyes.

Then as she stood outside the first one, feeling its cool shadows reaching out to her through the open door, she looked back and saw stretching away to the horizon was a view unlike anything she had ever seen or imagined.

It was a flat plain, broken by huge boulders and surrounded by low hills, and on every side of it a fortress of some sort silhouetted against the great arc of the sunlit sky.

It was so lovely, and at the same time Sita felt that it was not only its beauty she appreciated, but something leapt within herself to become part of it.

Even as it happened she thought that this was the spiritual feeling the man in the ship had promised she would find in India, and now she had.

After she had gazed at the view for a long time she walked into the Tomb first and remembered that Mr. Barnes had told her that there was a King buried beneath it.

There was a flat tombstone in the centre of the building under the dome, and as she looked at it she had the feeling that the dead King was watched over by those who had served and loved him when he was alive.

She went down some steps and up to the next Tomb, having a strange feeling that although they were empty, it was not the emptiness and loneliness of death, but that the spirits of the dead, or rather the spirits of life, were still there.

She reached the third Tomb which was away from the others.

Then as she entered it she saw that she was not alone. There was a man standing in a corner and because his face was in shadow she did not for the moment realise who it was, but only felt slightly annoyed that a stranger should interrupt the feelings that were intensifying within her.

They were so unusual that she wanted to savour them and not have them spoilt by having to speak politely to somebody else.

Then as if he spoke to her without words, she looked again at the man in the shadows and gave a little cry.

"It is you!" she exclaimed, "really you! I was thinking about you!"

"I heard you were coming here," he said, "and I wanted to see you."

"You heard? Who told you?"

"Does it matter?"

He came from the shadows and she saw that he was still wearing Indian dress. But she had the feeling, although she was too ignorant to be sure, that it was different from what he had worn in the ship, and now he appeared to belong to a different caste.

She had moved towards him as she spoke and he put out his hand to take hers and drew her out from the Tomb to a place where they were sheltered by a wall and which was also in the shade.

There was a stone bench on which Sita sat down and he sat beside her.

"Where have you been? What have you been doing?" she asked. "I thought perhaps I should see you in Calcutta. I was . . afraid once I had . . left I would never . . find you . . again."

He smiled and now because she was seeing him for the first time in daylight she realised he was very good-looking in a rather unusual manner.

As she had thought the first time she saw him his skin seemed darker than that of an Englishman, but in other respects it was difficult to know whether he was English or Indian.

She remembered her father saying once:

"After all, the Indians are Aryans like us, and while.

there are dark-skinned Indians, there are also light-skinned ones, and even Indians with blue eyes and fair hair. Their features and ours are more or less the same."

It was true, Sita thought now as she said impulsively:

"How could you leave the ship without telling me . . anything about . . yourself? I thought it was very . . unkind of . . you!"

"When the time comes I shall be able to answer that, and a great many other things as well," he replied. "But now I want to know about you. Are you enjoying yourself?"

Her eyes lit up and she said:

"You were right! Of course you were right, and everything is as . . wonderful as you said it would be. But there is so much more I want to know . . so much I want to . . learn . . and I feel that only . . you can . . teach me."

"Why should you think that?"

She looked away from him.

"I think it is because after you had . . saved me you made me . . think in a . . way I have never . . thought before."

"And that has helped you?"

"Of course it has, and it is very . . exciting!"

She paused before she said in a low voice:

"When I looked at the first Tomb here today I felt as if I . . understood what you had . . told me I would find in India . . which is something . . spiritual."

"That is what I always feel when I come here," he said, "and I would have been disappointed if you had found nothing but tombstones of Kings who have long-since died."

"I feel they are not . . dead," Sita said simply. "It seemed to me there was something . . alive in the first Tomb which I somehow . . cannot put into . . words."

"There is no need for you to do so," the man beside her replied, "in fact, it would be a mistake. What one feels in India can only be felt within oneself, and there are no words in which to describe it."

"But I also want to . . understand it in my . . brain."

"You will," he answered. "Now tell me what you think of the Residency."

"It is magnificent and full of love," Sita said impulsively.

The man laughed.

"I see somebody has been telling you of the story of the man who built it."

"It is very . . very . . romantic."

"And do you feel romantic?"

She looked away from him before she said a little shyly:

"Everybody has been very kind, but I cannot help feeling it would be more exciting if . . you were there to tell me the . . things I want to . . know."

"I am sure there are plenty of people to answer your questions," he said drily.

"There are, about the house and the city, but not about the real India which you told me existed, and which I am . . trying to find."

"Does it really matter to you?"

"I feel it is . . very . . important."

"Then it will be revealed to you, but as I said, you must have faith."

"I suppose that is what I am trying to find, but it is rather a . . dull name for something very . . different."

He laughed before he said:

"I know you are happy, and that is the first step in the right direction."

She thought of how she had told him she wanted to die, and blushed before she said:

"Are you still . . thinking I was very . . foolish and . . wicked?"

"I think you are now living up to your name and being brave."

"That is the nicest thing you could say to me, but I am afraid it was a compliment I . . fished for!"

There was silence, and because she was afraid he would leave her, Sita asked:

"When shall I see you again?"

"That of course is in the lap of the gods, but I do not think it will be very long."

She made a little sound of impatience as she said:

"I suppose you realise I find this secrecy very . . frustrating . . and I want to . . talk to you. I want you to . . teach me."

He gave what she thought was a sigh before he replied:

"There is nothing I can do about it at the moment. In fact, once again I am breaking my rules by coming here to see you. But I had to make sure you are happy."

"I am very happy," Sita said, "and very, very glad I have come to India, instead of disappearing into the Red Sea as I would have . . done if you had not . . stopped me."

"You are not to think about it," he said sharply. "It is something which did not happen, and please God never will."

There was silence. Then Sita said:

"I expect you know that when you save somebody's life you are afterwards . . responsible for them? That is why I am . . afraid that if you . . disappear I shall not be able to . . find you."

"We are in India now," he replied, "and I expect you have heard how the Indians use the power of thought so that they can communicate with anybody they wish to, however far away they may be."

"I have read about that, but is it really . . true?"

"Very true," he answered. "I remember once a man came to me to say that his father had died and he. must go back to his family immediately."

He paused before he went on:

"His father lived nearly two hundred miles away, and there was no possible means by which his family could have communicated with him."

"But you let him go?"

"It took a great deal of trouble to persuade his Superior, who had already refused his request, that he was not inventing some way by which he could obtain a holiday."

"So he went?"

"Yes, eventually he went and a week later I received confirmation that his father had died at exactly the time he had been aware of it."

Sita looked up at him wide-eyed.

"So what you are saying is that if I . . want you and it is . . really important I can . . tell you . . so?"

"Exactly. And believe that I shall not only hear you, but will come to you, if it is humanly possible."

As he spoke he rose to his feet and said:

"I think now you should go back to your escort. They will be wondering what has happened to you. Incidentally it would be better another time if someone like an *Aide-de-Camp* accompanied you."

"Why?" Sita asked. "There is nobody here, and if anybody frightened me, the servants are within call."

"Yes, I know," the man replied. "At the same time, those who stay at the Residency are usually chaperoned by the Resident's Staff."

Sita wrinkled her small nose.

"I am not used to such attentions and quite frankly I would find them rather intimidating."

The man laughed.

"You will grow used to it. What woman does not enjoy, if she is honest, pomp and circumstance which makes her feel like a very precious jewel?"

"Like a jewel," Sita said softly. "That is a lovely idea, and as jewels are something I shall never possess, it is intriguing to think that I myself am one."

The man did not speak but his dark eyes were looking at her in a way that made her shy, and because of it she said the first thing that came into her mind.

"My jewels are flowers from the gardens, and they are so lovely that I do not think even emeralds, rubies or diamonds could be any more decorative."

"Not on you," he said gently.

"I have only two gowns to wear in the evenings," Sita went on, "and I told myself I would look like a very poor little British sparrow beside the other ladies who are like peacocks, ospreys and birds of Paradise. But the flowers manage to make me feel proud, as you told me to be, and wearing them I no longer apologise for my poverty."

He did not speak, and she said quickly:

"I really should not be talking of my poverty when so many of the Indians are so desperately poor. I was horrified by those I saw in Calcutta and even here sometimes there are children with their . . ribs showing, and men and women who look . . hungry."

"They somehow manage to survive, but I am glad you noticed them, and realised that whatever their circumstances, they are still human beings."

"Of course they are!" Sita exclaimed. "I would like to help them, but as you well know, I am hardly capable of helping myself."

"I think you are doing very well," he said, "and shall I tell you that I am very proud of my pupil."

She looked up at him pleadingly.

"Do you really . . mean that? Or are you saying it . . just to . . please me?"

"I really mean it," he replied, "and now you must go back to your escort! But go on thinking and dreaming. It was what I expected, and I am not disappointed."

Because she knew he wanted her to go Sita looked at him a little indecisively before she asked almost like a child:

"You will be . . thinking of . . me?"

"Of course!"

He gave her a smile that seemed part of the sunshine, and she walked away from him through the open door of the Tomb and out at the other side.

There were two sets of steps to traverse before she reached the place where the horses were waiting.

She did not look back, thinking he would not want her to do so in case the two servants who were waiting for her might suspect that perhaps she had been talking to somebody while she was out of sight.

They brought her horse to the bottom of the steps so that they could serve as a mounting-block.

When she was in the saddle and had picked up the reins she moved slowly towards the gate through which they had entered, and her escort followed her.

Sita had no wish to speak.

All she wanted now was to return to the Residency thinking with a lilt within her heart that she had seen the man she wanted to see, and that he was pleased with her.

She could hear his deep voice saying:

"I am very proud of my pupil."

The words moved her, in the same way as she had been moved when she entered the Tomb for the first time.

Then as she asked herself why she should feel like that she was afraid of the answer.

Chapter Four

At breakfast next morning when Sita was alone with her uncle in their Sitting-Room, he seemed in a good temper so she asked:

"What do you think, Uncle Harvey, about Mr. Blunt's idea of Home Rule for India?"

Sir Harvey stiffened.

"Have you been listening to that intolerable windbag?" he asked sharply. "I suggest you find something better to do with your time."

"You think it is a mistake?"

"I think Blunt is off his head," Sir Harvey replied angrily. "He is trying to make trouble and God knows there is quite enough of it here already."

Sita wanted to ask what trouble there was, but thought it might annoy her uncle even more.

Then he went on:

"The Viceroy is almost as bad with his ideas of Indian Judges being allowed to try Europeans."

"You do not approve?"

"Approve? Of course I do not approve!" Sir Harvey snapped. "I have at least persuaded him to tone down some of the clauses in his ridiculous Bill."

Sita did not reply, and he went on:

"I have had to be tactful about it. A Viceroy is a Viceroy, whatever high-flown ideas he may have. I am only hoping the whole thing will die a natural death before it becomes law."

Because Sita was aware that she knew so very little about the political situation and this was the first time her uncle had ever talked to her about it, she thought it wise to say quietly:

"I am sure where legal matters are concerned, Uncle Harvey, no one knows more than you do."

"That is true, very true, and thank God those who advise the Nizam realise that."

Now Sir Harvey was looking pleased with himself again and because it was a state in which Sita wished him to remain, she was silent.

There was however an interruption as one of the *Aides-de-Camp* came into the Sitting-Room.

"Good morning, Sir Harvey, good morning Miss Arran," he said politely. "I have brought your programme for today."

He laid it in front of Sir Harvey saying:

"Mr. Cordery is hoping you can be with him in half-an-hour's time, Sir, as he has several of our legal advisors with him, whom he wishes you to meet and who, I may add, are very anxious to meet you."

"Thank you," Sir Harvey replied. "I suppose we are to talk in the usual room?"

"Exactly," the *Aide-de-Camp* agreed.

Then he looked at Sita.

"Mr. Barnes asked me to tell you, Miss Arran, that unless you have another engagement he would be delighted to take you in an hour's time round the Begum's garden, which he understood you would like to see."

"I am longing to see it!" Sita cried. "How very kind of him! Where shall I meet him?"

"He will come here to collect you, Miss Arran and I thought you would also like to know there is a large dinner-party this evening of about fifty guests with some of the leading Muslim noblemen present. There will be a short entertainment of Indian dancing."

"How exciting!" Sita exclaimed.

"After that the younger members of the party," the *Aide-de-Camp* went on, "might find it agreeable to dance in the small Ballroom."

"It sounds wonderful!"

"It will only be a small affair," the *Aide-de-Camp* smiled, "because we are keeping our big effort for when the Viceroy visits us in two weeks time."

"I am longing for that," Sita said, "and only hope we shall still be here."

She looked at her uncle questioningly as she spoke, and there was a pause before he answered:

"It all depends on how the negotiations go. If we make as slow progress as we have so far, I imagine we shall be here not only in February but also in March and April as well!"

The *Aide-de-Camp* laughed.

"I am afraid, Sir, you will find that the Indians agree today and invariably return tomorrow to disagree."

There was a faint smile on Sir Harvey's lips as he said:

"I have found that in the past, and it means that the hot-headed reforms of Mr. Wilfrid Blunt will at this rate take years or even centuries before they are put into operation."

"That is certainly true," the *Aide-de-Camp* agreed, "which is comfortably reassuring."

He laid in front of Sita an identical programme to the one he had given Sir Harvey, which detailed the hours of everything that was to take place, bowed to her, and walked towards the door.

Only as he reached it did he say:

"By the way, Miss Arran, I am sure you would like to know that the Nizam himself is calling here the day after tomorrow to discuss with the Resident the appointment of a new Prime Minister."

"Coming here?" Sita asked. "On an elephant?"

"He will ride one, and bring two others with him," the *Aide-de-Camp* replied with a smile and shut the door after him.

Sita clasped her hands together with excitement.

"Did you hear that, Uncle Harvey?" she asked. "I have been longing to see the Nizam and of course his elephants when they are all dressed up in their finery."

"You will find our host is not as enthusiastic as you about the visit," Sir Harvey remarked.

"Why not?" Sita enquired.

"It is too long to explain and you would not understand, but to put it briefly, Cordery wishes the young Nizam to choose a mature and sensible man as his new Prime Minister, but Blunt has been intriguing with the Viceroy to have some young whipper-snapper of twenty-two appointed."

As Sir Harvey finished speaking he rose from the breakfast table and moved to his desk.

The way he spoke told Sita that it was no use her asking him any more questions. At the same time they trembled on her lips and there were a dozen things she wanted to know.

Then she gave a little sigh.

"It is so frustrating," she told herself, "that nobody thinks women should be interested in politics. So I hear just enough to whet my curiosity and not enough to understand exactly what is happening."

She stood looking out into the garden, and inevitably her thoughts went to the only man who she felt could explain things clearly to her.

It was quite obvious there were two warring points of view in the Residency itself, of which one was leading what appeared to be at the moment a successful offensive against Mr. Cordery and his staff.

Although she was far too diplomatic to say so openly, she had the impression that the Resident and those who were older around him did not approve of Lord Ripon.

'What I want to know is which point of view is right for India.'

Once again she was thinking, as she had thought last night, that in the few moments she had been with her friend outside the Tomb there had been no time to talk of anything except herself.

She gave another sigh, then realised that the *Jemadar* or Senior Servant who waited on them was at her side.

"What is it, Amar?" she asked.

"The *darzi* here, Lady *Sahib*, awaiting your instructions."

"A tailor?" Sita asked. "There must be some mistake."

"No, Lady *sahib*, he have present, and ready make what you wish.

"I do not understand."

"Lady *Sahib* come see."

Amar led the way out of the Sitting-Room, and through an open door onto a small verandah.

Unlike most houses in India the Residency had few verandahs and those there were had been added long after Major Kirkpatrick's original plans.

There was however one outside the Suite of rooms which Sir Harvey and Sita had been allotted, and there she saw a small elderly man waiting.

He bowed low as she appeared, then held out a parcel wrapped in coloured paper and burst into a long dissertation.

"He say," Amar translated, "he brings for Lady *Sahib* one evening, one day-gown, he ask for pattern to copy."

"Who is the present from?" Sita asked.

Amar asked the question and in response there was a long reply which translated meant in four words that he did not know. He had just been told what to do which was to go to the Residency.

"Who told him to come here?"

The tailor had received instructions from another tailor who had given him the parcel and told him to hurry. That was all he knew.

Because she was extremly curious, Sita opened the parcel.

As she did so she gave a little gasp.

Inside there was first yards and yards of very beautiful material which she was sure an Indian lady would have made into a *Sari*.

The background was white and embroidered on it in real silver thread was a design which looked very much like small stars.

After one glance Sita had no need to ask who had sent it to her, and she felt embarrassed because thinking back on her conversation outside the Tomb she felt she had almost asked for a present.

At the same time, she was wildly excited to receive such a gift just when she was well aware how dowdy she would look at the Dinner-party and dance this evening.

As well as the material of silver and white there was another neatly folded roll of blue chiffon to match her eyes.

There was no need to measure it to know that while the cheap gowns she had managed to buy in England had very small bustles since to cut the cost the amount of material had been reduced to the minimum.

With what she had here she could have a bustle that would equal Lady Anne Blunt's or any other lady present tonight.

Because it was so thrilling to receive such a lovely gift and there was no possible chance of her refusing or returning it, she ran to her bedroom to bring back one of her evening-gowns and also her best afternoon one.

She was aware that they were both looking a little limp and the evening-gown was marked where she had pinned the flowers, which meant she would be unable to vary their position.

The *darzi* looked at them carefully, and she knew he understood exactly what was required. She explained to Amar that he must use as much material in the bustle as could be spared so that it looked large and important.

This produced a speech which appeared to go on and on endlessly until finally Amar said:

"He understand, Lady *Sahib*. He very good man. Best in town."

"I am glad to hear that," Sita smiled.

Then a frightening thought struck her and she said in a very different voice:

"What will he . . charge me for . . making these two gowns?"

Again the question and reply took time until Amar said:

"*Darzi* say material and making gift. No charge, Lady *Sahib*. He well paid."

Sita gave a sigh of relief.

Even though she knew her mother would not have approved of her accepting a present from a strange man whose name she did not even know, there was nothing she could do about it.

She appeased her conscience by arguing:

"He is not really a stranger. He saved my life, and that puts him in a very different position from what anybody else would be."

At the same time she knew that she wanted to thank him and it was infuriating to realise that she had no way of getting in touch with him except in her thoughts.

Mr. Barnes collected her and they walked towards the Begum's Garden where Major Kirkpatrick had built the small model of the Residency for the wife he loved and with whom he had been very happy.

To Sita it was beautiful, secluded, haunted!

She also felt perceptively that the love which Khair-un-Nissa had had for her husband had given the whole place an atmosphere which neither time nor a succession of other Residents could erase.

What she loved was the miniature Palace complete with portico and balustrade, but it was disappointing that Mr. Barnes would not let her go inside it.

Sita thought how much Major Kirkpatrick must have loved his Persian wife to have taken such trouble to amuse her.

Then once again she found herself wondering if today in the same circumstances she herself would have been so brave as to break the strict rule of *purdah* and tell an Englishman of her love.

Almost as if she was visualising their children running about in the secret garden with the little Palace in which to play she asked:

"Were the children of the marriage happy?"

Mr. Barnes smiled.

"It is a question I have often asked myself," he said. "Unfortunately I do not know the answer."

"I have always heard," Sita said hesitatingly, "that . . half-castes while very intelligent . . are often unhappy because they are not accepted fully by either their father's or their mother's families."

"That is true," Mr. Barnes agreed, "and as I can see you are a romantic, Miss Arran, we can only hope the Kirkpatrick children were the exception."

He paused before he added:

"And as you say a half-caste, or Eurasian, as we like to call them, is usually very intelligent."

As he spoke Sita suddenly thought that of course that was the obvious explanation for the man who had saved her life.

He spoke like an Englishman, so his father must have been English, but his skin was dark because his mother had been an Indian.

"Perhaps that is why he is so clever, and is part of 'The Great Game'," she reasoned.

She wanted to comfort him because he had perhaps suffered from his dual origin and sympathise with the conflicts which must have affected him ever since he had been born.

There were a great many other questions she wanted to ask Mr. Barnes but an *Aide-de-Camp* came towards them through the garden.

To reach them he had obviously hurried in the heat for he was breathless and there were beads of sweat on his forehead.

"What is it, Carstairs?" Mr. Barnes enquired.

"I was sent to tell you," the *Aide-de-Camp* replied, "that there is trouble in the Bazaar. Captain Robertson has gone off immediately with a platoon and the Resident thinks we should send information of what is happening to the Barracks just in case reinforcements are required."

"Yes, of course," Mr. Barnes said. "I will come and see to it."

He began to walk towards the main house with Sita beside him.

"What sort of trouble is it?" she asked.

"We have been fearing an explosion of some sort," Mr. Barnes replied. "There is tension between the Muslims and the Hindus, because someone we are not certain who, is to put it colloquially 'stirring things up'."

"It would not be serious, could it?" Sita asked, remembering the horror and terror that had occurred during the great Indian Mutiny.

Mr. Barnes shook his head and as if he was aware of what she was thinking said:

"No, no, it would be nothing like that. Just a bit of rioting between the extremists on both sides. It is unfortunately inevitable because of the many thousands of people over whom the Nizam rules four-fifths are Hindus."

"As many as that!" Sita exclaimed, then realised that Mr. Barnes was no longer listening.

She wondered if Wilfrid Blunt had anything to do with the trouble. Then it suddenly struck her that this might be the reason why her friend was in disguise.

Obviously '*The Great Game*' would be concerned with making sure that the peace of the largest Province in India was not disrupted.

'If only somebody would tell me exactly what is happening!' Sita wanted to cry out.

But as they reached the main door into the Residency, Mr. Barnes hurried away and she was left with nobody to talk to except herself.

* * *

The dinner party that night at the Residency was certainly impressive and just as in the Viceroy's house in Calcutta, there was a footman in white, scarlet and gold, known as a *Knitmagar* behind every chair.

The gentlemen wore their decorations and the ladies, whose gowns were resplendent, affected tiaras and a profusion of jewels which would have made Sita feel very dowdy had she not been wearing her 'present'.

Incredible though it seemed, the *darzi* had finished the evening gown for her to wear that evening, but Amar explained that he wished on the next day when he came to take her other gown to tidy off one or two of the seams inside.

"Lady *Sahib* wear tonight for big party," Amar said.

The way he spoke made Sita feel as if he was almost as pleased as she was that she would look so attractive.

It was, when she put it on, a dream-gown, such as she had always longed to possess.

Every time she moved the light shone on the silver embroidery and made her look as if she was dressed in stars.

The *darzi* had copied her own gown line for line, but as the embroidery of the material was stiffer, it swept out from her small waist and the bustle at the back was large enough to equal anything she had seen worn by any other ladies at the Residency.

Because she felt the low-cut *décolletage* looked some-how too bare, Sita tied a piece of white ribbon round her long neck and added a small white flower.

It gave her just the touch that was necessary!

With her eyes shining as brightly as the stars embroidered on her dress, she walked a little self-consciously beside her uncle to the Drawing-Room.

It was typical, she thought, that he did not notice that she was dressed differently from any other evening.

But he was in fact, looking very distinguished himself, wearing the Ribbon of a Knight Commander of the Star of India round his neck, and the Cross on his stiff white shirt.

He also wore on his coat the insignia of several other distinctions he had acquired during his years in India.

When the Resident appeared, stout though he was, he managed to look very impressive, and the Muslim guests, Sita thought, not only spoke very good English, but were obviously delighted to have been invited to dinner in the Residency.

Wilfrid Blunt had proclaimed at luncheon that he felt

happier in Hyderabad under the rule of the Nizam than in "the mournful towns under British rule, like Madras and Calcutta".

Because the Muslims could accept hospitality and eat with the English, Sita had learnt that it was very much easier to entertain them than the Hindus who considered their food was contaminated if even the shadow of an Englishman fell upon it.

Anyway the huge table which stretched the whole length of the Dining Room, lit with gold candelabra and decorated with a profusion of gold ornaments, many of them set with jewels, was so lovely that Sita felt she only wanted to look and not talk.

Nevertheless through politeness she made conversation with the gentlemen on each side of her, at the same time being frightened of missing something because she wanted always to remember the picture in front of her eyes.

After dinner they moved to the *Durbar* Hall where chairs had been arranged in front of a raised platform which made a stage.

There was first Indian music played on the *Mridangan* – drums – the *Nattuvangam* – flute. Then the dancers appeared.

The women wore the most elaborate dress and make-up and danced first the Nandana Gana Pathy which was in praise of God Genea – the god who removes all obstacles.

The movements were beautiful and Sita thought in future she would pray to Lord Genea to remove any obstacles in her life.

The next dance was Tarangam and described in mime episodes in the life of Lord Krishna, the god of love.

Sita thought the movements and the facial expressions were so vivid that they told the story just as eloquently as if it had been spoken in words.

While to her it was entrancing she saw that many of the English people were stifling yawns and the *Aides-de-Camp* were obviously bored, as if they had seen it too often before.

When the entertainment was over the Muslim guests said their farewells and the English moved to one of the smaller rooms which was to be used as a Ballroom.

There was a String Band playing the Waltzes with which Offenbach had captivated Paris, and there was also the traditional Lancers and Quadrilles.

Sita enjoyed every moment of it, and had more partners than there were dances.

Then when it was growing fairly late Wilfrid Blunt asked her to dance a waltz with him.

He was a good dancer, and she thought as many women had thought before that he was an extremely handsome man. However he had recently grown a beard, and she was convinced he would have been better-looking without it.

They danced several times round the Ballroom, then he drew her through an open window outside which was a path between the pillars with which the house was so profusely decorated.

As he started to walk down some steps into the garden, Sita said a little nervously:

"I am told that there are many flying foxes in the trees, and to tell the truth, I am rather frightened of them."

"I will look after you," Wilfrid Blunt replied.

He however did not go very far and she was still in the light from the house, as he said:

"I want to talk to you, Miss Arran."

"What . . about?"

There was a little pause as if he was seeking for words. Then he said:

"I am sure by this time you are aware of my feeling that India should be independent and have Home Rule."

"Yes, I am," Sita agreed.

"It is very gratifying that the Viceroy agrees to a certain extent with my views," Mr. Blunt said. "He has a great respect for your uncle, and so has Mr. Cordery."

He paused, then as Sita did not speak he went on:

"I know that you are not only very beautiful, but also very intelligent. May I beg you to try to persuade your

78

uncle to support me and give his blessing to the Ilbert Bill."

Sita was surprised at his request, and what was more she almost laughed out loud.

She could hardly believe that Mr. Blunt really thought she had any influence with her uncle.

Then she told herself there was no reason why he should have the slightest idea how much her uncle despised her or how when they were at home, a day never passed without his telling her she was a fool and hitting her for her mistakes.

It was only because here he was too busy with his endless interviews either with the Nizam's officials or with the Resident, that she had nothing to copy out for him and there was also one of the Resident's official secretaries at his disposal.

She was aware that because she had not replied Wilfrid Blunt was looking at her enquiringly.

Because she did not wish to argue with him and was also still asking herself whether she supported his ideas or not, she said tentatively:

"I am . . afraid I have very little influence . . with my uncle . . but I would like to know more . . about what you are . . trying to achieve and to decide whether it would really be the . . best for India."

"That is the sort of answer I want to hear," Wilfrid Blunt said, "and now I look at you and realise how lovely you are, it is quite unnecessary for you to be clever as well."

The way he spoke and the caressing note in his voice that had not been there before made Sita look at him in surprise.

Then to her astonishment he put out his arms and drew her close to him.

"I am willing to teach you about India, and even more willing to teach you about love."

As he spoke his lips came very near to hers and Sita realised with a sense of panic that he intended to kiss her.

It was so astonishing that he should want to and so unexpected that for a moment she felt it was impossible to move, almost impossible to think.

Then before his lips could touch her she twisted her head aside and started to struggle wildly in his arms.

"No . . no!"

"Why not?" he asked. "You excite and entrance me, and I want to kiss you, as I have wanted to do for some time."

"Please . . let me . . go!" Sita pleaded in a frightened little voice, her head still turned away. "You have no . . right to . . behave like . . this!"

"I have the same right as any other man attracted by a woman as beautiful as you," Wilfrid Blunt said, "and you look so alluring tonight, as if you were one of the stars in the sky."

His words made Sita think of how she had looked at the stars on the ship with her Indian friend beside her for a very different reason.

Then she was aware that she found Wilfrid Blunt repulsive!

She thought too it was extremely wrong of him to speak to her in such a way when he was a married man and his wife was dancing in the Ballroom.

With a sudden show of strength he had not expected, she forced herself free of his arms.

"Please . . leave me . . alone," she said.

Wilfrid Blunt was unabashed.

"Why should I do that?" he asked. "You are very lovely, Sita, like your name. To me you are the goddess to whom I wish to write poems, and kneel in worship at your feet."

"You should not be . . talking . . like . . this!"

She looked as she spoke towards the lighted room behind them and Wilfrid Blunt said:

"If you are worrying about my wife, forget it! She is very understanding and, if it is a scene you are afraid of, I promise you there will not be one."

Sita drew in her breath.

"What you have just said . . Mr. Blunt . . only confirms my conviction that you are behaving in a very . . reprehensible . . manner. If your wife does not object to your . . making love to . . other women, I do, and I will not . . listen to . . you!"

Wilfrid Blunt laughed.

"You are very young and very adorable when you are rebuking me! It is certainly a change from women who surrender too quickly."

He put out his hand and took hold of Sita's before she could move away.

"Shall I tell you," he said, "that I shall pursue you relentlessly? And because I am a very persistent lover, you will eventually surrender!"

The complacency with which he spoke and the note of passion in his voice frightened her.

Sita snatched her hand from him, and lifting up her skirts s..e ran away, climbing up the steps to disappear between two white pillars into the lighted Ballroom.

Wilfrid Blunt gave a little laugh which was not the sound of a man who was disconcerted.

He was well aware of his own attractions which had been successful in winning him the love of many famous and distinguished women.

When he was very young he had been the lover of the famous Courtesan 'Skittles', who had been the Queen of her profession and one of the finest horse-riders in England.

His other romantic affairs had usually been with aristocratic married women and marriage had not blinded his roving eye.

Lady Anne had more or less accepted that he would never be faithful to any woman for long.

He told himself now that Sita Arran was different in some way he could not exactly explain from any other woman to whom he had been attracted.

For one thing she was a young girl, and he had seldom, if ever, looked at girls.

For another, there was something romantic about her

which was not only part of her mind or what women invariably referred to as their heart, but in the very air she breathed.

He found himself watching her at mealtimes and when she walked into a room.

Although he told himself he was making a mistake when engaged on his important crusade to liberate India, he found himself desiring her and until tonight he had been certain that she would surrender herself to him eagerly.

Wilfrid Blunt was conceited with reason and by now was very sure of himself as a lover. He was surprised, but not in the least disconcerted by Sita's resistance.

He was only sure that his impression that she had never been kissed was true, and there was no man in her life.

'She will be mine before we leave here,' he thought.

There was a smile on his lips and a look in his eyes which his wife recognised as he walked into the Ballroom pondering how he could get Sita alone, and when he did, make sure this time that she did not escape so easily.

*   *   *

Sita was not only shocked at Wilfrid Blunt's behaviour, but also a little afraid.

Because she was so inexperienced where men were concerned, she had no idea how to handle one who made passionate advances to her, least of all, a man who was married, and as much in the public eye at this present moment as Wilfrid Blunt.

"How can he behave in such a manner?" she asked herself.

She wondered if he pursued her, as he said he would, what she would be able to do about it.

The last person she could turn to for help would be her uncle, who would only assume that it was her own fault, or since he so much disliked Wilfrid Blunt, she had encouraged him and might make a scene which could result in their having to leave Hyderabad immediately.

The whole idea of having to go back to England was so upsetting that Sita felt almost like crying at the idea.

For the first time since her parents had died she was being treated as a human being, and living in a manner that in the past had been only part of her dreams.

To leave all this and return to the gloom and unhappiness she had found in Wimbledon would, she thought, be like being transported to penal servitude.

However badly Wilfrid Blunt behaved, her uncle must not have the slightest idea of it, and somehow she would have to cope with him herself.

Then she knew that there was one person she must tell: one person whose advice she must ask.

She was quite certain that just as he had saved her, guided her, and helped her to become a very different person from what she had been before, he would know what she must say and how she must cope with Wilfrid Blunt.

'I must see him! I must see him at once!' she thought. As she danced around the Ballroom with one of the *Aides-de-Camp* she saw Wilfrid Blunt come in from the garden.

Because she was frightened, he seemed taller than he had before and she felt he definitely menaced her.

She could still feel the strength of his arms and how afraid she had been that she would not be able to fight herself free of him.

Then when he had taken her hand she had been unable to prevent it.

She thought with a little quiver that if he had taken her further into the garden and kissed her by force there would have been nothing she could do about it.

"I hate . . him! I . . despise him!" she said beneath her breath.

She was so horrified that what she was feeling communicated itself to her partner and he asked:

"You are looking worried. Am I treading on your toes or has something upset you?"

"No . . of course not! It is . . none of those . . things," Sita managed to say lightly. "I was just wondering what . . happened at the Bazaar."

As this was the same *Aide-de-Camp*, Lieutenant Carstairs, who had brought the news of the trouble to Mr. Barnes, he knew what she was talking about.

"I imagine everything is settled by now," he replied, "but these things get out of hand if they are not stopped promptly!"

"What did . . happen?" Sita persisted.

"I have not heard the whole story myself," the Lieutenant replied, "but apparently, there is some chap who is inciting the Hindus to rebel against Muslim rule, and making it a religious problem."

He laughed before he added:

"As everything is religious in this country, it invariably ends in bloodshed."

"I hope that will not happen," Sita cried.

"Not if we can help it," Lieutenant Carstairs answered, "and our troops are pretty experienced at this sort of thing."

He swung her round several times before he said:

"The trouble is, if one puts out a fire in one place, another flares up somewhere else. At the moment it is all due to this fellow we cannot catch."

"Who is he? What do you know about him?"

"Absolutely nothing!" the Lieutenant confessed. "We just know he is there, or we think he is! He is supposed to have arrived recently, but it is no use asking me for the answers because I am in the dark like everybody else."

It was then Sita was certain there was one person who would know: one person who was following or trying to find the trouble-maker.

She danced around the room in silence before she asked:

"Was there much . . fighting in the . . Bazaar?"

"I think half-a-dozen people were killed," Mr. Carstairs answered lightly, "and a number of others were wounded, but nothing more is likely to happen tonight, at any rate, with our sepoys on guard."

Because she was frightened by what she heard, Sita wanted to enquire who had been killed and what were their names. Then she knew it was a stupid question.

Even if Lieutenant Carstairs gave her a list of the names she would be none the wiser.

It was then she knew that tomorrow she must go to the Tombs again, just in case he was there.

Surely, she told herself, if she sent out the waves of thought he had told her were so effective, he would be aware that she wanted to see him and would come to her?

He had been so certain that was the way in which she could contact him, and now she would try to prove it.

The dance came to an end and as she deliberately walked in a different direction from where Wilfrid Blunt was standing she saw Mr. Barnes coming from the side of the Resident as if he had some instructions to carry out.

Impulsively, Sita ran towards him.

"Please, Mr. Barnes, I want to ask you something."

"What is it?"

"May I go riding early tomorrow morning? I was so thrilled with the Tombs of the Kings yesterday, that I want to see them again. In fact, I actually visited only three of them."

Mr. Barnes smiled.

"Then you have four more to go! Yes, of course, Miss Arran, I will order the horses to be ready for you at the same time as yesterday, if you will not find that too early after a late night."

"As a matter of fact," Lieutenant Carstairs said who had been listening, "we are not going to be very late. I see His Excellency is retiring now, which means we will all have to go to bed."

"And I must do my duty," Mr. Barnes said. "I was just going to tell the Band to play 'God Save the Queen'. Excuse me, Miss Arran, I promise everything will be arranged for your ride."

He hurried away, and a moment later everybody stood to attention to the strains of "*God Save the Queen.*"

It made a very impressive picture and one that would have excited Sita's imagination, had she not been intent on sending her thoughts to the one man who she hoped would listen to them.

Chapter Five

Sita lay awake most of the night worrying about Wilfrid Blunt, and at the same time terrified in case one of the people who had been killed in the Bazaar was her friend.

And yet, something told her that if he was dead she would have known it and she was sure with an instinct that could not be denied that he was alive.

She lay there in the dark calling to him for help, and feeling because he had been so positive that they could communicate with each other in that way, that he would hear her.

Almost as soon as the sun brightened the sky she rose, and was dressed long before the horses were waiting for her outside.

She wrote a note for her uncle to say that she had gone riding, then after a quick breakfast she ran to the side door with an eagerness which she would not suppress.

The same two men who had accompanied her before made her an obeisance at her appearance, and when she was in the saddle they mounted their own horses and rode after her.

Because Sita was in a hurry to reach the Tombs she set off at a quicker pace than yesterday, and for once was not moved by the silver beauty of the Musi River.

Nor was she interested in the deer in the Park, the flock of *Guyarat* cranes with their huge span of wings, the herd of buffalo which she had learnt with amusement provided the milk for the house.

Instead she was anxious to leave the city behind and see the gigantic bare boulders which would tell her she was nearing the Tombs.

They passed the Barracks, and the country was wild

and very beautiful until they neared the large Garden, where the Tombs were situated.

This she had learned from Mr. Barnes was called *Langar Faiz Asar*.

He had also told her that the most important Tomb and the most impressive was that of *Muhammad-Quli Qut'h Shah* the founder of Hyderabad, and she thought she would look at it more carefully on this second visit.

At the same time she was well aware that she would be hurrying to the third Tomb where she had met her friend before.

Because she was excited at the thought of seeing him and was confident he would be there at her first glimpse the gardens with their colourful flowers seemed even lovelier than before and she quickly dismounted.

As she walked up the steps to the first Tomb she saw her escort take the horses as they had done before under the shade of a tree.

Because she had no wish for them to think that she was doing anything unusual, she passed through the first Tomb and the second.

Then with a light in her eyes that her Indian friend would have recognised as being the same as when she had looked up at the stars, she hurried to the third where he had been waiting for her.

Because she had been so certain that he would be there, when she found the Tomb empty and there was no one in the shadows the disappointment was as sharp as a physical pain.

"I am early," she reassured herself. "He will come, I know he will come!"

She waited for a little while in the Tomb, then thought she would go on to the ones she had not had time to visit before.

There were four of them, one being quite near to where she was.

Slowly, because in a way she was reluctant to leave the Tomb where he had been waiting for her, she stepped out onto the plateau on which each Tomb was erected and looked for the steps which would carry her down to ground level from which she must climb again to reach the next Tomb.

The sunshine was blinding, and she walked carefully on the steps, afraid of slipping since through age and the ravage of weather they were broken and cracked and in consequence dangerous.

She had just reached the ground when suddenly it seemed as if a man or an animal sprang at her from where he had been lying hidden below the plateau from which she had just descended.

Sita gave a scream of fear, and as she did so something dark and enveloping was flung over her head, and while she gasped at the shock of it, she felt it wound round her and she was lifted off her feet.

There were two men to carry her, and although she tried to struggle, her arms were pinioned to her sides, and her voice was lost against the thickness of the material which enveloped her.

After two or three efforts to shout for help she realised she had hardly any air and was afraid she might suffocate, as it was only with difficulty that she could breathe.

Then she knew she was being carried quickly and that her captors must be on a smooth path.

She guessed that she was being carried through the gardens and knew she was right in what she surmised when after they had moved for quite some way, they stood still and as once again she tried to scream, there was a sound of wheels.

A moment later she was bundled into the back of a carriage and immediately the horses which drew it were driven off along what Sita knew was the dusty road outside the big stone gateway which led into the garden.

She thought that the two men who had carried her were seated on the small seat opposite where she was lying, but they did not speak and she could only feel that they were there and watching her.

It was then she tried to reason out what had happened,

and could find no possible explanation for her being carried away in such a strange manner.

She supposed she had been kidnapped but why and by whom?

It would not be for money, for there were hundreds of people in Hyderabad who were worth a fortune, while the English who lived and worked in India were as a rule not rich men, unless they were in some high position.

"Why? Why has this happened to me?" Sita asked and could find no answer.

They drove quite a long way along a very rough road on which the carriage rocked over stones and holes and the horses were forced to go slowly.

Her face was still covered by a blanket or similar material which was so thick that she again began to fear she might lose consciousness through being unable to breathe.

There was no question of being able to scream and she could only lie, feeling terrified, and at the same time praying desperately that she would not be hurt.

It seemed incredible that anyone from the Residency should be kidnapped for a ransom or any other reason, and she could not imagine how in any way she could be playing a part in the troubles between the Muslims and the Hindus.

The carriage drove on and on, until the horses were climbing up hills and zig-zagging as if to make it easier.

Finally they came to a standstill, and astonishingly, although she could hardly believe it, Sita heard a man's voice ask in English:

"You've got her?"

"Yes, she's here."

"Very well, pick her up and follow me."

She was lifted from the carriage, and now the men who were carrying her were climbing over rough ground, stumbling occasionally against the stones so that Sita was afraid they might drop her.

And they were English!

She thought she must be mistaken. Why should the English kidnap her?

There seemed to be no possible reason for it, and in a way because it was so incomprehensible it made her even more frightened.

Then the man who had given orders before said:

"Take her down slowly. The steps are broken and can be dangerous."

Now from the angle at which she was carried, Sita realised she was being taken down some steps which made the men holding her stop and feel every now and then for a foothold.

"What is happening to me?" she asked and began to pray frantically because it was so weird and mystifying that she wanted to scream and go on screaming.

Then the steps came to an end and now they were walking on flat ground for a short distance.

They stopped, and there was a sound of a door being scraped open.

"Take her inside," the man said who was giving the orders, "and cover your faces before you release her."

Sita held her breath and made a little effort to struggle, but it was impossible to move, and she felt herself lowered not too gently onto a bed of some sort.

There was a pause, and she was wondering if she could pull off the blanket which enveloped her when it was lifted from her body and thrown back off her face.

Because she had been in complete darkness, at first all she could see was a dark roof over her head.

Then as her eyes grew accustomed to the light which was coming through what appeared to be a hole high up in a stone wall she saw there were three men standing and staring down at her.

At first glance they seemed terrifying because they had handkerchiefs over the lower part of their faces, leaving only their eyes.

She attempted to sit upon what she realised was a kind of bed.

"What . . are you . . doing? Why have . . you brought . . me here?" she asked.

She meant to sound accusing and angry, but instead her voice was weak and very frightened.

The tallest of the three men, who when he spoke she realised was the man who had given orders, answered:

"We have brought you here, Miss Arran, to make sure that your uncle gives the right advice to the Viceroy who we understand had consulted him with regard to the Ilbert Bill."

"The Ilbert . . Bill? What has . . that to do . . with me?"

"If your uncle wants you back, he will have to agree to kill it."

Sita gasped and sat up to stare at the three men confronting her in sheer amazement.

It flashed through her mind that they must be mad.

Then she remembered that most Europeans were violently opposed to the Viceroy's idea of giving the Indian Judges jurisdiction over them, and these Englishmen were trying by any means they could to make Lord Ripon change his mind.

It all seemed so incredible and so far removed from common sense that she could hardly believe it was happening.

Yet apparently she was a prisoner, and now she thought she might have guessed it before that she was in the Golconda Fort.

Because they were waiting for her to speak, she forced away the weakness that made her feel faint to say hesitatingly:

"I . . I think that my uncle has already . . advised the Viceroy to . . modify the Bill which is . . worrying you."

"That's not what we've heard," the tall man replied, "and Sir Harvey had his chance when he was in Calcutta to tell the Viceroy that we English will not stand for such an imposition."

He spoke angrily and as Sita did not answer he added:

"Anyway, he will doubtless take more notice when he finds you've disappeared! We will only take you back to him when he agrees to oppose the Bill publicly so that there will be no doubt in anyone's mind as to his attitude."

Sita pushed her hair back from her forehead and realised it was wet.

She had been wearing a hat and she supposed it must have fallen off when they had thrown the blanket over her head.

Then she said in a voice that trembled:

"Supposing . . my uncle does not . . agree?"

"Then you will stay here until you rot or die of starvation!" one of the men said fiercely.

"How can you do . . anything so . . wicked?"

"It's nothing to what the Viceroy and your uncle are trying to do to us," the third man said who had not spoken until now.

"I'm not going to argue with you, Miss Arran," the tallest man interposed. "We're only informing you of your position, and if you do die it will doubtless be in a good cause."

"But surely . . you understand this is . . nothing to do with me?" Sita pleaded. " . . Whatever I said to my uncle . . he would not listen."

"He'll listen to us," the man retorted, "and we have to make him and the Viceroy realise that they have a mutiny on their hands, and this time it is from the English."

As he spoke he walked out of the cell, for it was nothing else, and the two other men followed him.

The door slammed shut and Sita heard them put a bar across it, which sounded like a very heavy one.

Then as she put her hands up over her eyes she realised she was trembling.

How could this have happened to her?

The more she thought about it, the more she realised that in a way it was understandable that the British who had had their own way in India for so long would dislike reforms however necessary they might be or whoever proposed them.

There must be many men like her uncle who had no wish for progress of any sort and would resent, as he did, any innovations, especially if they took any of his power or authority from him.

'Of course Uncle Harvey is against the Bill,' she thought, but added that if Wilfrid Blunt was for it, then it must be wrong.

At the same time she was not certain. No one had ever explained the pros. and cons. to her, and she had had no time to ask the only man whose opinion she valued.

As she thought of him, she sent out a cry for help that seemed to come from the very depths of her being, and involved not only her brain, and her heart, but also her soul.

"Save me! Save me!" she cried.

Then she thought despairingly that he would never find her.

She had wanted to ask him to help her to defend herself against Wilfrid Blunt.

Never had she imagined in her wildest dreams that she would be kidnapped by Englishmen and carried away by force to a Fort which had proved impregnable in the past, and would undoubtedly again prove impregnable where she was concerned.

There was silence outside her prison door and she knew the men had left her and gone.

She rose from where she was sitting and looked around to see if there was any way by which she could escape.

She was in what was obviously a cell and presumably in the past had been used as a dungeon or a prison for malefactors.

It was small and the walls were made of grey stones just as she supposed the whole fortress had been.

The only light came from the opening she had noticed at first which was high against the ceiling.

Now looking up she saw that even if she could climb up there, which was unlikely, there were three rusty iron bars which told her she had been right in thinking it was a prison cell.

The door was stoutly made of wood, but there were new hinges which were oiled and she thought they had been added recently when the men had decided to bring her here as their prisoner.

Now that she was standing she looked down at where she had been lying and saw it was a native bed, which was simply four wooden feet with a mattress made of twine.

There was also, she saw, in the corner a jug which contained water and a glass.

There was nothing else, except for the blanket in which she had been enveloped, and she thought despairingly that they certainly did not intend to make her comfortable.

She touched the walls and found the stones were cool and she thought her prison would be cold during the night because most of it was below ground level.

Then she sat down again on the bed and tried to think what she could do.

She was almost sure that however skilfully she argued with the Englishman they would not listen to her.

They did not quite have gentlemanly voices, but they were not common men, and she thought that as the senior of them had quite a good vocabulary they perhaps had either industrial or official positions of some sort.

This would account for their anger at contemplating that they might be tried in the Law Courts by Indian Judges.

At the same time, because it all seemed so fantastic and something that could never happen in England, Sita could hardly believe it was true.

Then as the silence seemed to creep over her and make her more afraid than she was already, she was aware once again that only one person could save her.

But how would he know? How would he ever learn that she was missing?

She reasoned that it might be a long time before the two grooms who had escorted her to the Tombs would become worried when she failed to appear.

Indian servants never queried their orders, and because she had told them to wait they would wait. It might be two or three hours before they started looking for her, and only when they could not find her would they wonder what had happened.

She tried to calculate how long it would be before they would take the initiative and return to the Residency to report that she was missing.

This in fact would be the last thing they would want to do because they would be accused of not protecting her properly, but she supposed that eventually, perhaps late in the afternoon, they would be forced to return.

Then she remembered that the Englishmen had said that they would notify her uncle that she had been kidnapped in which case Mr. Barnes who knew where she had gone might send soldiers out to look for her.

Even so it would not occur to them that she had been carried off to the Fort.

She had already learnt how large it was, and even if they did come here to search for her it would take them a very long time.

"What can I do?" Sita asked despairingly, and knew the answer was – nothing!

She then frightened herself by thinking that if her uncle received the communication addressed to him to say she had been kidnapped and on what terms she would be released he might, if he was in one of his bad moods, simply do nothing about it.

He was always unpredictable where she was concerned, and she had the terrifying feeling that he might see it as a good way to be rid of her, justifying himself at the same time on principle that he would not be bullied into doing anything he did not wish to do.

"He may be against the Bill," Sita told herself, "but he would loathe and detest being pressurized by what is really blackmail into opposing the Viceroy publicly."

The whole thing was such a muddle and so incomprehensible that she put up her hands to her face and wanted to cry from sheer despair.

Then almost as if he was speaking to her she could hear her friend say;

"You must be proud and brave, like the goddess after whom you were named."

"How can I be proud when I am here?" Sita asked as if she was arguing with him, "and if I am brave, who is there to impress?"

She looked up at the window. There was a shaft of sunshine coming through it and she longed to be free.

She had thought the grey misery of her uncle's house in Wimbledon utterly depressing, but at least she could move about there and be in the open air, and not be afraid that she really would be left to starve.

The hours passed slowly. Then with a sudden constriction of fear Sita heard voices and footsteps coming slowly down the twisting steps.

There was the sound of several men talking amongst themselves, the bolt on the door was raised, and they came into the cell.

There were now eight of them, and they all had handkerchiefs tied over the lower part of their faces.

But as they were hatless she could see that three were grey haired, two were going bald, and the other three she thought, were young and perhaps not more than twenty-two to twenty-five years old.

They stood looking at her in silence until she asked defensively:

"What . . do you . . want? Why are you . . staring at me?"

"We just came to see what you looked like," one of the younger men replied, "and all I can say is if I was your uncle I wouldn't want to lose anybody so pretty!"

They all laughed at that, and one of the other men said:

"That's typical of you, Archie, but she's important to us for other reasons."

"I know that," Archie replied, "but I've still got eyes in my head!"

The other man who had given orders when she had first arrived pushed forward to stand in front of her and say:

"I thought you would like to know, Miss Arran, that your uncle has been informed that you are in our hands. Perhaps tomorrow or the next day, if he has not responded, we will get you to write to him, but in the meantime, I suggest you pray that he sees sense, and quickly."

"I can only hope," Sita replied, lifting her chin, "that you realise how abominably you are all behaving, and whether you are taken in front of an English Judge or an Indian one, kidnapping must involve severe legal penalties."

They seemed to be surprised into silence by the way she spoke. Then Archie laughed and said:

"I'll say one thing for you – pretty lady – you've got guts! I'm sorry now we can't make you more comfortable."

"That is enough, Archie!" the older man said sharply. "It would be a mistake for us all to hang about here. Go back to Headquarters, and there will be two of you on guard during the night at three-hourly intervals before you are relieved."

"Bags I the first watch!" Archie said. "I hate being woken up once I've gone to sleep."

Some of the men laughed at this and were teasing him as they moved out of the cell.

As they reached the door Archie looked back and Sita thought the way he was staring at her was insulting.

She lifted her chin, hoping because she had confronted them and not shown how afraid she was her Indian friend would have been proud of her.

Then she wondered if he would ever know.

Suppose she was never found? Suppose as one of them had said she was left to rot here and starve to death?

They had not brought her any food and, although she had longed to ask for something to eat, she would not give them the satisfaction of saying 'no'.

When she heard them going up the steps again she had the idea that they were deliberately keeping her hungry.

Then if she had to write to her uncle a pleading letter she could tell him in the message that she was being starved.

"It is despicable! How can an Englishman do anything so unsporting?" she asked angrily.

It was obvious that the English thought and behaved in a very different way from how they would at home.

Once again she was asking what she should do, and knew the only answer was that she must try, as she had tried before, to send her thoughts towards the only person she was certain could help her.

The day wore on and because she was indeed exhausted by all that had happened and had slept very little the night before, Sita dozed for a short while during the heat of the afternoon.

She was not sure if it was a dream, or whether it was his thoughts coming to her, as she tried to send hers to him, but she could almost hear his voice saying:

"Believe that I will not only hear you, but I will come to you if it is humanly possible."

"I do believe," she answered, "and I want you . . I want you now! Come to me . . please come!"

In her dream he was beside her. Then as she put out her arms towards him she awoke with a start, and there was only silence except for the caw of the crows outside.

The sun was losing its warmth and Sita knew it would not be long before it was dark.

She could hardly believe that they really intended to leave her without food and without a light.

She drank a little of the water and lay down on the bed, listening and waiting.

She was suddenly afraid to sleep because of snakes, rats, and civet cats which she had been told in Calcutta came through the windows of the Viceroy's house.

Then she remembered that if any of these invaded her solitude she would be able to call for help from the guard outside.

Because it was so eerie being alone, she was even glad

when she heard their footsteps coming down the stairs, and knew that Archie and another man were arriving on sentry duty.

After so many hours of solitude, the mere fact that they were talking English was somehow reassuring. Then there was a knock on the door and Archie asked:

"Are you all right, Miss Arran?"

"Yes . . thank you."

"We are here to prevent you from escaping, so if you want to talk to us, we can come inside."

"No . . no," Sita said quickly. "I am . . going to . . sleep."

"All right then – pleasant dreams!"

"Thank you."

She sat down on the bed and as she did so realised that Archie and his companion had brought a lantern with them.

She could see the light from under the door and also on the sides of it where the wooden frame to which it was attached did not fit, or where the stones had crumbled away.

Because she thought she might be able to see what they looked like without them concealing handkerchiefs, she slipped off her shoes and walked silently across the floor in her stockinged feet towards the little spots of golden light.

At a first look she was unable to see anything, but she tried another hole and she now could see the two men sitting on the floor, their legs stretched out in front of them.

By the light of the lantern which cast a golden glow over the area outside the door of her prison she could see that Archie was dark with a small moustache, and he looked somewhat flamboyant and in a common way, rather handsome.

The man with him was nondescript with fair hair and spectacles, and might be a senior Bank Clerk, or perhaps the manager of some Industrial Concern.

"I call this damned uncomfortable!" he remarked to Archie, "and if you ask me, that Lawyer chap won't give in easily."

"Simpson is quite certain he will," Archie replied, "and there's no other way we can make them take any notice of us."

"No, I suppose not," the other man said somewhat drily, "but quite frankly, I would rather be at home sleeping comfortably in my own bed.

"I thought, Brian, you'd be the one to complain," Archie said scornfully. "What I'm thinking is that our prisoner is a jolly pretty girl, and I'd like to get better acquainted with her!"

"There will be trouble if you do that."

"With – Simpson?"

There was silence, and as Archie glanced towards the barred door, Sita drew in her breath.

After a moment, as if he made up his mind, he said:

"I'll tell you what I'm going to do, Brian. I'm going back to see if all the others have settled down, and get myself a drink. I can't think why we didn't bring one with us."

"What do you want a drink for?" Brian enquired.

"Because I'm thirsty," Archie replied. "I thought, too, I'd bring one for her."

He jerked his thumb as he spoke towards the door they were guarding and added before his friend could speak:

"Nothing warms a girl up like a drop of gin, and if you think I'm going to sit here on this hard stone for the next three hours – I'm not!"

"If you start playing about with her she may make a fuss."

Archie laughed.

"Who to? I'm not going to harm her. A kiss and a cuddle never hurt any woman!"

"I don't know what Simpson will say," the other man protested.

"Oh, don't be so chicken-hearted," Archie replied.

"Come on, we both need a drink, then we'll have a good time. I've not seen anything so pretty in a month of Sundays!"

They got to their feet and then as Sita could see that Archie was making towards the steps which were behind them, Brian said:

"We'd better take the lantern with us."

"Don't be stupid!" Archie answered. "We don't want to be seen. We'll creep there. There'll be light enough from the stars, besides there's a moon tonight. We'll get ourselves a couple of bottles before Simpson or anyone else is aware that we've moved from our post."

"All right," Brian agreed. "I'll leave it to you."

"I thought you would," Archie said, his voice fading into the distance as he climbed the steps.

Sita was trembling from what she had heard.

She knew she had no defence against two men, especially when one of them was a man like Archie.

If she had been frightened of Wilfrid Blunt kissing her, she was much more terrified of what these men would do.

Every instinct in her body cried out against the idea of being touched or kissed by such men.

To be in their power would be so degrading and humiliating that she wished she could have died before this should happen.

"How can I bear it?" she cried.

Moving from the door she sat down on the bed to cover her face with her hands.

She was praying frantically, desperately. Then as she repeated over and over again: "God, help me! Please, help me! Do not let them touch me!" she heard the bolt being lifted off the door.

Her whole body stiffened and she held her breath.

Surely they could not have returned so soon?

But there was no doubt that the door was opening slowly, and now there was the figure of a man silhouetted against the light outside.

She got to her feet, wanting to hide, wanting to run and having nowhere to go.

Then without being able to see his face she knew who was there and that her prayers had been answered.

With a little cry that was somehow smothered in her throat she ran towards him to fling herself against him.

"You .. have come! You have .. come!" she said frantically. "I have been .. praying that you would .. and now .. you are .. here!"

Her voice was almost incoherent.

His arms went around her and he held her very close.

"It is all right, my darling," he said, but she hardly heard him.

"They are .. coming back .. they have gone to get .. some wine .. They said they would .. touch me .. and kiss me .. oh .. save me .. please .. save me!"

He did not answer, but he merely pulled her through the door, and then outside in the light from the lantern turned back to shut it and put the bar across it back into place.

Then taking her hand he drew her towards the steps.

Sita could understand as she climbed them the difficulty the men had had in bringing her down them, but the hand that held her was strong, sustaining, and so comforting that she was no longer afraid.

He drew her out of what she saw was little more than a hole in the ground. Then there was the starlight, and a moon moving up the sky to light their way.

He did not say anything, but only set off moving quickly over the rough ground, past the rubble and stones which had once been part of the fort, skirting the bushes which had grown among the ruins and drawing Sita behind him so confidently that they were both moving swiftly and surely.

Only after they reached what Sita was aware was the top of the fort did they start to go down again.

How it was difficult not to slip on the rough grass, or fall over what had once been a defending wall which was now almost buried, and a danger if they went too fast.

Then when they seemed to have walked for a long time and Sita knew they were right on the far side of the fort from where her prison had been, she saw in the shadows of the trees there was a horse tied by its reins to a branch.

As they reached it she said, speaking for the first time since she had left her prison:

"You . . came! How could . . you have . . found me? How can I tell . . you what it . . means that you are . . here?"

She looked up at him, and because she was so thankful to be saved her voice broke, and there were tears in her eyes.

She thought he looked at her for a long moment before he put his arms around her and held her close. Then his lips were on hers.

To Sita it was no surprise, it was what she realised now she had longed for although she had not been aware of it, and it was so infinitely wonderful that he had saved her from humiliation and degradation, if not worse.

As his lips held her captive, she felt as if the stars moved into her breast and were in her heart and her mind, and also on his lips.

He kissed her until she felt she was no longer herself but his, and it was so wonderful that it was impossible to think of anything except that she loved him and he filled her whole world, and she was no longer afraid.

When he raised his head, she was still too bemused and enraptured to speak. He picked her up in his arms and put her on the saddle of his horse.

Releasing the reins he mounted behind her and giving the animal his head set off in the direction from which she knew she had come.

She could feel his left arm around her, holding her close against his chest, and she put her head with a little sigh against his shoulder.

She was thinking it impossible that she should have been transported so swiftly into a Heaven of happiness from a hell of terror and despair which now by a miracle was behind her.

Only when she could find her voice after the wonder of

his kiss did she manage to ask in a little more than a whisper;

"How .. did you .. find me?"

"How can you have gone to the Tombs alone when I told you you should have somebody responsible with you?" he asked.

"I .. I forgot what you had said .. because I wanted .. so desperately to see you .. and I was sending my .. thoughts to you all .. last night."

She looked up at him as she spoke, and thought that his dark eyes in the moonlight looked stern and she said a little nervously:

"Y.you are not .. angry with me?"

"I am angry with those responsible for you at the Residency that they could not have looked after you better."

"But .. how could you have guessed .. how could anybody have known .. that I would be .. kidnapped by the English?"

There was silence. Then she asked.

"Did you know that was who had taken me away?"

"I heard your uncle had received a letter threatening him."

"Who could have told you that?" Sita asked.

Then before he could reply she added:

"Who could have known last night that I was .. coming to the Tombs to .. find you?"

She felt his arm tighten around her as he said:

"Everything is known in India. Surely you are aware by this time that it is impossible to have secrets? News is carried on the wind, in the sky, and in the earth, and everything that happens is known almost as soon as it occurs."

"And .. you knew about .. me?"

"I was worried about you," he said, "and I had the feeling that you needed me."

"I .. needed you desperately .. but for a different .. reason, but tell me first how you found me?"

He smiled.

105

"When I heard you had been kidnapped, I guessed where they would have taken you, and I was right!"

"Did you tell . . them at the . . Residency?"

"No, I came to find you."

Sita thought from the way he spoke that he was afraid no one would listen to him, or else he had no wish to communicate with the Residency.

"I . . I was afraid for . . you when I heard there had been . . fighting in the Bazaars," she said impulsively. "I was desperately . . worried in case you were . . hurt or . . killed."

"I think if I had been killed you would have known," he said quietly. "As I knew last night that you needed me."

"Did you . . guess I would go to the . . Tombs?"

"I thought you might," he said, "but it is impossible for me to get there so early, and by the time I was free I had heard what had happened to you."

She wanted to ask him what he had been doing that he could not answer her first call for help.

Then she knew that he would not answer her questions, but would only tell her what he wanted her to know.

Anyway, everything else was immaterial beside the fact that she was safe, she was in his arms, and he had kissed her.

She looked up at him and said very softly:

"I . . I love you!"

He looked down at her, and she could see his face in the moonlight and felt his eyes were looking down into her soul.

"Are you sure of that?"

"I am as . . sure of it as I have been . . sure of . . anything in . . my whole life."

"And I love you!" he said very quietly.

He bent his head and just touched her lips, but she felt as if the moonlight swept through her like a streak of lightning.

They rode on and Sita was thinking that because he

loved her nothing mattered. Even if he was very poor and she had to live in an overcrowded slum or in a tent, it would still be like living in Heaven.

"What are you thinking?" he asked.

"I was thinking of . . you . . and how . . much I . . love you."

"If you love me, another time you must obey me," he said. "I do not remember ever being so frightened as when I heard that you had been kidnapped, and nobody in the Residency had the slightest idea what they could do about it."

"What have they . . done?"

"I believe they have sent soldiers to search for you."

"An Englishman called Simpson said that if Uncle Harvey did not do what they wanted, I could rot in the prison to which they had taken me or . . starve to . . death!"

She thought that he nodded his head, as if that was what he expected. Then he said:

"You must be very hungry, my darling, and I am going to take you to the Barracks so that they can drive you home."

"I do not want to leave . . you!" Sita protested.

"I know," he answered, "but it will not be very long now before I can be with you. In the meantime, you have to trust me and promise me you will do exactly what I tell you."

"Then we can be . . together?"

"As soon as I can arrange it."

His arms tightened as he said:

"I do not think I could lose you now."

"I was so . . afraid of . . losing you," Sita replied, "and before you leave me . . there is . . something I want to . . say to you."

"What is it?"

"I . . sent my thoughts out towards you last night . . because I was . . frightened of . . Wilfrid Blunt."

"Of Blunt?"

"Yes. He tried to . . kiss me and said that I would not be able to . . escape from him for long . . and I was frightened!"

"Damn the man! He is an infernal nuisance!"

Because he was speaking in the same way that her uncle had, Sita have a little laugh.

Then she said:

"It does not matter now. I will manage somehow . . but please . . can I be with you very . . very soon?"

She paused to rest her head against his shoulder and said:

"What I was going to say was . . if we have to be very . . poor or face a lot of opposition from Uncle Harvey . . or anybody else . . promise that you will not leave me . . and that nothing will matter . . except that we . . love each other."

She wanted to add that if he was an Eurasian, as she suspected, it did not matter, and if his family was as angry as her uncle would be, that would not matter either.

Somehow she was aware that he knew what she was trying to say, and he kissed her forehead before he said:

"I adore you for what you are thinking, my precious one, but I promise you that nothing and nobody will prevent me from looking after you and protecting you for the rest of your life."

He gave a little laugh as he said:

"It may be quite a task, and certainly I did not expect to combat kidnappers, but I anticipated you were far too lovely to escape the attentions of the Wilfrid Blunts of this world."

"He frightened me, but now I am not even frightened of having to . . starve to death because I know that you . . will save me."

"Please God, that is the truth."

She moved a little closer to him before she asked:

"I cannot leave you now that you have said you love me, without your telling me how I can think of you. It is so difficult to think about anybody or pray for them if they are completely anonymous."

He laughed before he answered:

"Very well, but you have to give me your promise that you will not speak about me until I tell you that you may. For one reason, it might be dangerous."

"For you?"

"Perhaps."

"Then you know I would never in my wildest dreams do anything that might hurt you! I love you! I love you so much that I want to . . protect you and make . . you happy."

"My precious, that is what I feel about you," he said, "and very soon I will be able to protect you completely and nothing shall ever frighten you again."

As he spoke he pulled the horse to a standstill underneath the shadow of a great banyan tree and let the reins fall loose on the animal's back while he put both his arms around Sita and held her close before he kissed her.

His kisses were fierce and demandingly possessive, and she felt as if her whole body melted into his and she was a part of him, and they were no longer two people, but one.

Only when he raised his head did she say in a voice she had never used before, but which had a touch of passion in it:

"I love you! I love . . you . . and there are . . no other words in which I can tell you how much . . you mean to me!"

He did not reply. He merely kissed her again until when she felt as if her whole body was pulsating with the wonder of it he said very quietly:

"This is where I have to leave you, my precious one. I want you to walk down the road, and you will see two sentry-boxes. Tell them who you are, and ask to be taken immediately to the Commanding Officer."

He knew without her saying so that she was a little nervous, and he added:

"I will wait here until I am certain that you have been taken into the Barracks, and are being properly looked after."

"You . . promise?"

"I have told you to trust me."

Sita gave a little sigh.

"You . . know I do . . that!"

"Then everything will be all right, my darling."

As he spoke he dismounted, and lifted her gently to the ground.

For a moment he held her close against him again, and kissed her forehead but not her mouth.

Then because she knew what he wanted her to do, she walked slowly down the road towards the sentry-boles, aware as she reached them that the soldiers were staring at her in astonishment.

Chapter Six

Sita awoke early despite the fact that she had been late going to bed.

There had been so much excitement in the Residency when she was brought back in a carriage by the Commanding Officer from the Barracks, that she found herself the centre of attention in a way she had never been before.

Not only did the Resident want to talk to her, but her uncle had a great deal to say, and was simply furious that any man who called himself an Englishman could behave in such a manner.

She did as her friend had told her and only said she had managed to escape from her prison, and walked to the Barracks which they considered in itself an achievement.

"It is a long way, and you must have been very frightened," Mr. Barnes said admiringly. "It was certainly very brave of you."

"There was nothing else I could do," Sita replied.

Then she quickly changed the subject to other matters.

She knew that before she left the Barracks the Commanding Officer sent out a number of soldiers to arrest the Englishmen if they were still in the fort when they arrived.

Although there was a great deal of talk about what would happen when they were captured, Sita had the idea that when Archie and Brian realised she had escaped they would know, since the bar was on the outside of the prison door, that somebody had released her, and they would leave as quickly as possible.

This ultimately proved to be the truth, although Sita did not learn of it until late the following afternoon.

Mr. Barnes made notes of everything she told them before they finally allowed her to go to bed.

Only when she was alone was she able to think of the wonder of the kisses she had received, and the rapture in her heart because she loved somebody who loved her in return.

It was then she remembered that she had been so bemused by his lips and the loving things he had said to her that she still had no idea of his name.

Also that she had forgotten to thank him for her gowns.

It had been impossible to think of clothes when all that was in her mind was that she was safe, and he had saved her.

"He is so wonderful!" she told herself before she fell asleep, and the same words were in her mind when she awoke.

Going back over what they had said to each other she realised he had not actually asked her in so many words to marry him.

She had just supposed that was what he intended when he said he would look after her, protect her, and they would be together.

A little flicker of fear made her wonder if because of the difference in their situations and perhaps even in their nationalities, he did not intend her to be his wife.

Then she knew, almost as if he had told her so, that their love was greater than caste, colour or nationality, and she already belonged to him in everything except name.

"I love him! I love him!" she told the sunshine coming through her window.

She felt as if the words were carried towards him in the magical way that Indians could communicate with each other.

He had told her to trust him, and she knew she did so, though at the same time, she could not help wondering about him and how he managed to be so well informed.

There must be somebody at the Residency who had

communicated with him when the kidnappers' letter had been brought to her uncle.

She wondered if any of the servants were in his pay, or if, as he said, everything that happened in India was carried on the wind.

But all that really mattered was that he had come to her when she needed him most, he had saved her, and she knew that never again would she leave the Residency without being properly protected.

Mr. Cordery had in fact been extremely annoyed about it.

"Why was Miss Arran allowed to go and visit the Tombs without you or one of the *Aides-de-Camp* escorting her?" he had asked Mr. Barnes.

Mr. Barnes looked embarrassed.

"I am extremely sorry, Sir, and I admit now that it was very remiss of me. But it seemed such a short and simple journey, and we were, if you remember, extremely busy yesterday with the rioting in the Bazaar."

"What I want you to do," Sir Harvey interposed, "is to catch these men, and if there was ever a good reason for having them tried by an Indian Judge, this is it!"

The Resident looked at Sir Harvey in consternation.

"I hope, Sir Harvey, that is not going to be your attitude in the future," he said. "You know my feelings about the Bill, and if this is the sort of reaction we are going to get over India, all I can say is that it will grievously affect the morale of the whole country."

"There I agree with you," Sir Harvey said in a different tone of voice, "and I think you should inform the Viceroy of what has occurred before Mr. Blunt gives him a biased account of it."

"That is exactly what I intend to do," the Resident said, "and Mr. Barnes, I want no details of what has occurred communicated to Mr. Wilfrid Blunt. This is a matter on which we do not want his interference."

"No, of course not, Sir," Mr. Barnes replied.

They would have gone on talking for hours if Sita,

despite the fact that she had been given something to eat and drink at the Barracks, was so tired that even her uncle noticed the pallor of her face and that she lay back limply in her chair.

"You had better go to bed, Sita," he said abruptly.

As if the Resident was aware of how exhausted she was he rose to his feet.

"Before I say goodnight, Miss Arran," he said, "I want to tell you how much I admire your bravery and initiative in being able to escape, and also the courage you have shown since you returned to us."

It was what they had said also at the Barracks, and Sita was feeling somewhat embarrassed at their praise, knowing she had not been as clever as they thought.

She knew in fact that if she was courageous now it was because she was so happy.

When she was alone in her bedroom she felt as if once again she held the stars to her breast, and they were also on her lips, as they had been when he had kissed her.

Now as she rose to look out on a golden world, she thought it was reflected in her heart, and that everything was so glorious that she felt as if she was part of the sun itself.

Now she need no longer be afraid of having to return to Wimbledon to endure her uncle's anger and cruelty.

Now she was no longer alone as she had been since her father and mother had died.

As she had said to the man she loved even if they had to live in a slum or a tent, as long as she was with him she could ask for nothing more.

It was only as she started to dress she remembered that the Nizam was coming this morning to call on the Resident and that was something to which she had been looking forward.

Because it was an official visit he would be riding on an elephant, rather than as he had on other occasions in a yellow coach and four, with postillions dressed in yellow and syces in the same.

When she went downstairs to wait for his arrival in the Durbar Hall where everybody else was assembled, she was aware that Wilfrid Blunt was looking pleased with himself, while those who were in attendance on the Resident had a somewhat grim expression on their faces.

She did not have to actually be told that the young applicant for the position of Prime Minister, Salar Jung, was in the lead, and it was unlikely that he would lose to Mr. Cordery's nominee, before the Viceroy arrived.

She was certain, however, that whoever was appointed, it would mean hours of talk, consultation and argument, and she was thankful that being a woman she did not have to be present at the meetings.

Sir Harvey had however been invited, and win or lose, as far as the Resident was concerned, he was delighted that they wanted his opinion and that to all intents and purposes he was back in the Seat of Judgment.

At breakfast he hardly spoke to Sita, but that was nothing new.

She knew that in his usual egotistical manner he was thinking of what lay ahead this morning, and he had dismissed any predicament she had been in yesterday from his mind.

That was certainly something she welcomed. At the same time, she knew how different her parents' reaction would have been to what had happened.

They would have worried in case what she had been through had not only upset her emotionally, but made her feel ill.

To her delight, when she was nearly dressed she found in her wardrobe the blue gown which the *darzi* had been making up yesterday.

It was even lovelier than she had expected. The blue made her skin dazzlingly white, and seemed to be a reflection not only of her eyes, but of the sky.

"It was dreadful of me to forget to thank him when he had been so kind," Sita murmured.

But she felt herself thrill as she thought when she did

115

see him again she would put her arms around his neck and thank him with her lips against his.

Then when she looked at herself in the mirror, she wished she could not only send her thoughts towards him, but also a picture of how she looked at this moment.

She was thinking of him all the time the young Nizam, a slim, good-looking man, was being received in the Durbar Hall.

He had arrived, as Sita knew, on an elephant, gorgeously arrayed in a jewelled harness, and accompanied by two other elephants.

She was disappointed not to be able to watch them proceeding through the crowded streets where she had learnt that every window and balcony would be filled with spectators, the Nizam's own troops keeping back the crowds.

"It is a gayer and more picturesque scene than most Indian crowds create," Lieutenant Carstairs told her, "because the men nearly all carry arms and accoutrements."

"It seems strange they should allow them to have firearms," Sita remarked.

She remembered that her father had told her that in other parts of India the English refused to allow the natives to own weapons of any sort.

"You are in Hyderabad now," Lieutenant Carstairs answered, "which is an Independent State, where all the nobility have large retinues and private troops, and armed forces of their own. Although that might seem dangerous, we only occasionally have any violence, like the other day in the Bazaar."

"It is certainly very different from what I expected," Sita remarked.

"Wait until you see the excitement when the Viceroy arrives," Lieutenant Carstairs smiled.

Then he left Sita in order to perform some social duty at the other side of the Hall.

When the welcoming ceremony was finished the Resident, the Nizam and Sir Harvey, together with a number

116

of Muslim nobilities, moved into a smaller room where they could start their discussions.

Sita longed to be able to go outside and look at the elephants, but she was told that those inside the building were expected to wait in the Durbar Hall until the Nizam left.

This did not worry her unduly, except that she thought it was rather a waste of time.

Mr. Blunt paced up and down in a temper and those watching and listening to him knew it was not only because they had to stay where they were, but also because on the Resident's strict instructions he had not been invited to the talks.

"They can talk all they want," Sita heard him say," but you mark my words, I shall get my own way and when Lord Ripon arrives, Salar Jung will be appointed Prime Minister."

Sita had managed to sit as far as possible away from him and Lady Anne.

At the same time, although she was now safe in the Residency from the kidnappers, she still had to cope with him. She only hoped he would be too piqued at being left out of the discussions to worry about her.

Far sooner than anyone had hopefully anticipated the Resident and the Nizam returned to the Durbar Hall.

Everybody stood as they proceeded slowly down the centre side by side, then followed in a procession.

Sita, seeing Wilfrid Blunt thrust himself in front of several people so that he could walk as near to the Nizam as possible, thought he was not only very pushy, but bad mannered.

Then as she longed to tell him to behave properly Mr. Barnes whispered in her ear:

"Come with me. I know you want to see the elephants, and I will take you to a good vantage point."

She smiled at him, and he took her through a side passage which led them onto the portico with its huge columns by a different entrance from the centre door which was being used by the Resident and the Nizam.

It was then that Sita saw with delight what she had been expecting, and knew they were even more exciting and glamorous than she had imagined.

Drawn up in front of the twenty-two white marble steps with huge Sphinxes on either side were a number of the Nizam's troops and in front of them were three elephants.

They stood there gorgeously arrayed with gold and jewels, and the centre one had a gold howdah on its back and a gold umbrella to shade the Nizam from the sun.

Because he was young and looked attractive, Sita could understand the wild enthusiasm that came from the crowd as soon as he appeared on the portico with the Resident beside him.

The cheers continued as the two Rulers said goodbye to each other formally, and the Nizam walked slowly and with dignity down the white steps.

Then as if they could contain their admiration and delight no longer, the crowd surged forward, thousands of them coming through the main gate. Even if the troops had wished to stop them, it would have been quite impossible to do so.

As the rest of the party from the Residency were moving down the steps, although Mr. Cordery stayed on the portico, Sita went with them.

They were now lining the steps to the ground level and the Nizam walked slowly past them.

He recognised one of the Residency officials and stopped to say a word to him, and he also patted the head of one of the English children who had been pushed to the front to present him shyly with a little bunch of flowers.

It was all rather touching. Then because the crowds has encroached almost to the steps Sita found herself looking at the cheering faces for just one person.

She felt somehow he would be there, and she hoped that if he was and could see her he would be pleased not only by her appearance, but that she was not too overcome by the events of yesterday to put in an appearance today.

"I want him to think me brave," she told herself and searched amongst the dark faces for the one that she knew would make her heart leap.

The cheers were almost deafening as the Nizam reached the last step and stood raising his hand in acknowledgement while the elephant in front of him went down on its knees.

It took a little time and the Nizam waved first to the crowd in front then to the left and to the right.

Sita was among those on the right, feeling that if the man she sought was there the vibrations that existed between them would draw her eyes to his.

Then suddenly a man in the front row of the crowd who was only a few yards from the Nizam put his hand inside his open shirt and drew out a pistol.

He did it unobtrusively and swiftly, but at the same time as he levelled it at the Nizam, Sita had time to scream: "Look out! Look out!" and pointed towards the assailant.

Because her voice was shrill and she was speaking in English the Nizam heard her and turned his head.

As he did so somebody sprang from the crowd and threw himself on top of the man with the pistol a split second before he pulled the trigger.

As she watched it happen Sita knew with her instinct as well as with her heart and her eyes who it was who had forced the man to the ground and was now struggling with him.

The crowd behind the two men seemed paralysed but she ran forward and bending down snatched the pistol from the assailant's hand.

Only as she took it away did the troops who were behind the elephants move and two *Aides-de-Camp* come running down the steps.

By this time the man on the ground was lying still, and the man who had thrown him down turned away as the troops reached them and was swallowed up in the screaming crowd.

Sita stood as if turned to stone, the pistol in her hand, unable to breathe or think.

As the unconscious man, or he might have been dead, was lifted up and carried away, somebody, she thought it was Lieutenant Carstairs, took the pistol from her hand, and taking her by the arm drew her back towards the steps.

It was then that the Nizam, who had not moved since she had shouted at him, but had watched what happened calmly as if he was not personally involved, said with a smile:

"I am very grateful to you, Miss Arran. I think because you saw my assailant before anybody else did, you saved my life."

He bowed and before Sita could reply climbed into the howdah on the kneeling elephant.

As he rode away with the two other elephants just a few paces behind him the crowd who had learnt what had happened went wild with delight.

Their screams, their yells drowned even the Band which preceded the procession and as the crowds surged after their Ruler, by the time Sita had reached the top of the steps the front of the Residency was almost empty.

Mr. Cordery, who had watched everything, hurried to her side to say:

"That was magnificent, Miss Arran! I cannot imagine what would have happened if the young Nizam had lost his life, which he might have easily done."

Sita did not reply, she merely smiled at him rather weakly and the Resident said sharply:

"Take Miss Arran somewhere where she can sit down and give her a glass of champagne. She certainly deserves it."

It was only after the champagne had taken away the feeling of faintness that had overcome her that Sita realised that she had been upset not only by the thought of the Nizam being murdered, but because the man she loved had been in danger.

She knew then that what had made her run and snatch

120

the weapon had been the fear not that the Nizam might die, but the man who was saving him.

'It is something we have done together,' she thought, and had no answer when Mr. Barnes said:

"I think, Miss Arran, you must have been the only person present who was watching the crowd rather than the Nizam. I have often warned our soldiers that when they are guarding somebody of importance it is from the crowd that the danger comes."

"I think you were magnificent!" Lieutenant Carstairs said, and there was an admiring look in his eyes which Sita knew was very flattering.

Everybody praised her until she felt a little guilty because she had not been thinking of the Nizam, but of somebody very different.

She had guessed already what was the reason for the attack, and it was confirmed when she heard the Resident say to Mr. Barnes:

"I presume the man was a Hindu?"

"Yes, of course, Sir, and I am quite certain he was acting on the instructions or at the instigation of this man who has been inciting the Hindus against the Muslims. But we shall know more when he is interrogated."

When she had a chance to speak to Mr. Barnes alone, Sita said:

"Please, when you find out more about the . . man who tried to shoot the Nizam, will you tell . . me what you have learned about him, and the . . person who is behind . . all the trouble?"

"I can understand your being curious," Mr. Barnes replied, "and of course, Miss Arran, I will tell you everything I can."

Because she did indeed feel somewhat shaken by the whole incident and did not wish to talk about it any more, Sita lay down after luncheon and actually slept for a little while.

Her uncle had gone once again to a meeting, but this time at the Nizam's Palace, and Mr. Barnes came to see her.

"How are you?" he asked.

"I am perfectly all right, thank you," Sita replied, "and feeling very lazy at having rested for so long."

"I think you were splendid!" he said. "I do not know of any woman who would behave so calmly after what you have been through, both yesterday and now today."

Sita did not reply, and he went on:

"I have news for you."

"About the assailant?"

"Yes. Of course it is secret, although after the way you saved the Nizam's life, I think you are entitled to receive some information, however confidential."

"Thank . . you."

"The man, as we all knew, was a Hindu, and he had been instructed to shoot the Nizam when he left here by the agitator who has been making trouble ever since he arrived."

"Where did he come from?" Sita asked.

"Originally from Russia."

"From Russia!"

She remembered as she repeated the words, what her father had said about the Russians being the enemy, and that they wished to oust the English and conquer India for themselves.

"The man we questioned," Mr. Barnes went on, "has told us that he entered the country not from the North, as we might have expected, but by ship."

Sita stiffened.

"He embarked either at Alexandria or Port Said, and arrived in Calcutta with one idea, and one idea only."

"Which . . was?"

"To put the whole of the Muslim population against the Hindus which would certainly have been achieved if their Ruler had been murdered by a Hindu."

"I can see it was a clever idea," Sita murmured.

"The difficulty has been," Mr. Barnes continued, "that nobody except one person had any idea what he looked like, and we were warned that while he was being watched it would be impossible to arrest him unless we could pin some crime directly onto him."

Sita was sure she knew who the 'one person' was!

"And you have . . managed to do . . that now?" she enquired.

Mr. Barnes nodded.

"The man who attempted to shoot the Nizam was persuaded to talk and the agitator has now been arrested and is in prison."

Sita clasped her hands together.

"I am glad . . so very . . glad!"

As she spoke she was almost certain this meant that the mission in which the man she loved had been involved was completed.

She was not quite certain how she knew, and yet the whole pattern of what had occurred ever since she had tried to drown herself, and he had prevented her, made it all fit into place.

She had been sure before they reached Calcutta that he was somehow involved in '*The Great Game*' and now it was confirmed.

She could only be grateful from the very depths of her heart that now he would be free, and not only would she learn who he was, but their love need no longer be a secret.

In a voice that did not sound like her own she said:

"What is the . . name of the . . man who shadowed the . . Russian?"

To her surprise Mr. Barnes stiffened. Then in a perceptably different tone of voice, he said quickly:

"I am afraid I have no idea! Just some Hindu I expect, who is in the Police Service, and more astute than the majority of them."

"An . . Indian?"

"The only way one can ever get near these troublemakers is to be able to speak their language fluently, and make them believe they have another disciple for their cause."

"Yes, of course," Sita said in a low voice.

Mr. Barnes drew his watch from his waist-coat pocket.

"Now I must get back to work," he said. "There is no need for me to tell you, Miss Arran, that what I have told you is not to be repeated to anybody else, and especially not to Mr. Wilfrid Blunt."

"Why him . . especially?"

Mr. Barnes smiled.

"Shall I say that not only does he turn everything to his own personal advantage, but he is also much too greedy."

He laughed before he added:

"I am quite certain he is at this moment extremely annoyed that neither he nor his wife was in your place to take the plaudits you so richly deserved."

Because of the way he spoke Sita could only laugh, and when he left her she sat deep in thought, only afraid that her dreams might not come true.

*   *   *

An hour later, when she was trying to read a book but finding herself unable to concentrate on it, Mr. Barnes came to the Sitting-Room again.

He was holding a box in his hand, and there were two servants behind him carrying a huge basket of flowers and very large garlands with which Indians decorated those of importance.

"This is from the Nizam, Miss Arran," he said. "His representative would have liked to see you, but I told him you were resting, so they entrusted to me what they had brought you."

As the servants put down the flowers and garlands and left the room he said:

"Incidentally, and I am sure you are glad, I have saved you from a long speech of gratitude which would have had to be translated and undoubtedly would have taken a long time."

"Thank you," Sita smiled.

Mr. Barnes put the box into her hands.

It was covered with silk, embroidered in very much the

same way as her gown, only this embroidery was gold and the box bore the Nizam's insignia in the centre of it.

"It is so pretty!" Sita exclaimed.

"Open it, and see what is inside," Mr. Barnes suggested. "I have a feeling you are going to be both surprised and delighted!"

Sita did as he suggested, and when she opened the lid of the box she saw that inside lying on a bed of velvet was a necklace that made her gasp.

It was of diamonds, set in the exquisite enamel which she knew was so characteristic of Indian jewellery.

The centre diamond was so large that she could hardly believe it was real, and if so, must be worth a fortune.

"I cannot . . accept this!" she said.

"It would certainly give great offence to the Nizam if you refused it," Mr. Barnes advised, "and there is no other way in which he can express his gratitude at being alive."

"I . . I did not . . really save him," Sita said. "It was the man who threw his assailant to the ground, and prevented him from . . firing at the . . Nizam."

"If you had not shouted when you did," Mr. Barnes contradicted, "and alerted the man who was watching him, he would have killed the Nizam. You deserve this present, Miss Arran, and a great deal more besides. Everybody feels so very very grateful to you."

"B.but . . it must be worth a . . fortune!" Sita faltered, looking at the necklace.

"The diamonds in it come from the Nizam's own mines which are not very far from the city, and I only wish I could show you the magnificent jewels which he owns."

"Are you . . really saying . . that I can . . accept this?" Sita asked in a low voice.

"It is something you must do," Mr. Barnes replied, "and may I add, Miss Arran, it will become you more than anybody else I know."

Sita blushed at the compliment, then Mr. Barnes turned towards the door.

When he reached it he turned back to say:

"Incidentally, it seems poetic justice that diamonds have been associated for many years with the Golconda Fort. A great number have been dug up in the Quth Shahi territory."

When he had left her, Sita put out her fingers wonderingly to touch the large diamond amd knew there was only one person she wished to see her wearing it: somebody with whom she must share it.

When her uncle returned to the Sitting-Room and she showed him what the Nizam had sent her, he said:

"It is certainly very impressive, but far too grand for you to wear. The best thing I can do with it is to sell it when we return to England, and you can spend the money on something sensible."

With difficulty Sita bit back the cry that the necklace was hers, and she had no intention of selling it. But she knew this would only antagonise her uncle, and it was better for the moment to agree with him.

Without saying any more Sir Harvey went to his bedroom to change for dinner, and Sita thought that his interview with the Nizam had not been as pleasant as he had expected.

She wished he would confide in her and tell her what was happening, but then she knew that Mr. Barnes had told her the only thing she wanted to know.

If the Russian was in prison, then the man who had been tracking him down could relax and feel free to do what he wished.

It was all supposition on her part that that was why the man who had saved her had been travelling steerage on the P. & O. ship, why he had not told her his name, and had even said it might be dangerous for her to know it.

Because there was no other way in which she could reach him, she sent out a cry not for help, but of love.

She felt he must know that she was not only thinking of him, wanting him, but aching and yearning for the moment when she would be in his arms again.

"I love you! I love you!" she said beneath her breath.

as she stood at the window and watched the shadows under the trees lengthening.

"I love . . you! I want . . you to . . come to . . me!"

Because her cry was so intense she almost felt as if he might materialise in front of her as he had done before.

But there was only the sound of the crows going to roost and far away in the distance the music and the noise of people who were still joyfully celebrating that their Ruler had been saved from death.

After a long time Sita turned from the window.

Now the sinking sun turned the large diamond in the necklace which she had left in its box open on the table, to a golden fire.

For a moment she looked at it, then thought that she would give up all the diamonds in the world and all the jewels in the Nizam's Palace for one kiss from the man she loved.

*   *   *

At dinner that night, to which a number of guests had been invited, among them two distinguished Muslims, Sita realised that her position in the Residency had completely changed since breakfast.

Now she was seated for the first time on the Resident's right with the most important Muslim on her other side.

The manner in which everybody had greeted her made her feel that she had been propelled into a leading part on the stage and nothing was quite real.

Because she thought it was expected of her, she wore the necklace the Nizam had sent her because it would have seemed bad manners not to do so.

She was also quite certain that everybody in the Residency would know by now what she had received.

Because it showed it off better than the sparkling gown she had worn last night, she put on one of the plain and simple ones she had bought in England.

It did not distract attention from the glorious necklace with its centre diamond, and was therefore on this occasion, at any rate more suitable than anything else she possessed.

She knew as soon as she entered the Drawing-Room where they all assembled before dinner that it was difficult for the women to raise their eyes from her neck and Lady Anne said somewhat acidly:

"It is certainly a most adequate reward for one little scream!"

"I am very grateful for His Exalted Highness's generosity," Sita replied quietly.

She tried to avoid Wilfrid Blunt, but was unsuccessful.

He walked up to her, and in a low voice which only she could hear said:

"You are far too beautiful to need such baubles! Your eyes shine more brightly than any diamond, and your lips are more alluring than the rubies in your necklace!"

Because he frightened her she wanted to move away without speaking, but felt those near them might think it rather strange, so instead she said in a formal, frigid little voice:

"How very kind of you, Mr. Blunt, to be so complimentary!"

She then looked towards her uncle and said:

"Please excuse me, but I think Uncle Harvey wants me."

She realised as she left him that Wilfrid Blunt was merely amused and she was sure he was finding her resistance to his charms positively provocative.

"I hate him!" Sita told herself.

At the same time she was not as frightened of him as she had been yesterday, though she still felt that he menaced her.

When dinner was over and the gentlemen joined the ladies in the Drawing-Room, Wilfrid Blunt deliberately walked towards her and sat down beside her.

"I am sure you will be glad to know," he said, "that I am writing a poem in praise of your action today, which when we are all dead will remain as a memorial to your courage."

"How very . . kind of . . you."

"In the meantime," he went on, "I want to quote to

you some lines I wrote several years ago, but which are very applicable at this moment."

Sita wished to say that she did not want to listen, but she had the feeling that Lady Anne was watching them from the other side of the room, and it might be awkward if she guessed what her husband was saying.

Wilfrid Blunt bent forward to look into Sita's face and said in his deep voice which, while she hated him, she had to admit was well-toned:

> " . . . that through my chase . . .
> I seemed to see and follow still your face.
> Your face my quarry was. For it I rode
> My horse a thing of wings, myself a god."

He finished, then he said quietly:

"Your face is my quarry, and I have no intention of giving up the chase."

"Then you . . will be . . disappointed."

As she saw he did not believe her she said as quietly as he had spoken:

"Perhaps I should be frank with you and tell you I am deeply and . . overwhelmingly . . in love, and you will . . understand in the circumstances that I just wish to be . . left alone."

"You are in love?" Wilfrid Blunt asked sharply. "I do not believe it! With whom?"

Sita did not reply and he said:

"It cannot be anybody here and I learnt from your uncle that you live very quietly when you are in England and meet few people."

"Why should you question my uncle about me?" Sita asked.

"That is a rather stupid question," Wilfrid Blunt replied. "You must be aware that everything you do and say interests me, and every minute I fall more deeply in love with you than I was a moment before."

She was sure that he had spoken in this manner dozens of times to a great number of women, and because she felt his complacency was infuritating, she answered:

"Since you know a great deal about love, Mr. Blunt, you must be . . aware that when one's . . affections and one's . . whole heart are fixed on one . . person, every other man . . pales into . . insignificance."

Because even to think of her friend made her feel braver than she had ever been before, she added sharply:

"Please . . leave me alone! I dislike you . . Mr. Blunt, and quite . . frankly, I find you repulsive!"

As she spoke she rose to her feet and walking across the room to where Mr. Cordery was sitting talking to a very attractive woman, she said:

"I hope you will not think it rude if I retire to bed. I am afraid the dramas of the day have left me with a headache."

The Resident struggled to his feet.

"That is not surprising, Miss Arran," he said, "and once again let me thank you for saving us all from a very uncomfortable situation. It is something which might have had far-reaching consequences, not only in this Province, but over the whole of India."

"You are very . . kind."

Sita curtsied. Then without saying goodnight to anybody else she went from the room.

Only as she came out of the Drawing-Room and walked along the corridor which led to their rooms did a servant appear with a note on a gold salver.

"Just come, Lady *Sahib*," he said.

Sita took the note wondering who had sent it and thinking perhaps it was one of congratulation from somebody in the city.

She did not open it until she reached her own bedroom.

Then as she saw the cheap piece of paper inside the envelope contained only five words her heart gave a sudden leap and she read and re-read them.

Just five words, but they said all that she wanted to hear:

"Trust me. I love you!"

Chapter Seven

"I must see you alone."

"It is . . impossible!"

For three days Sita had been striving to avoid Wilfrid Blunt and had been successful, but now unexpectedly she found herself sitting next to him at luncheon.

It was being given for a politician who was passing through Hyderabad, and Sita had felt apprehensive when she had sat down to find Wilfrid Blunt beside her.

She had known he was delighted, and she was aware intuitively that he had been feeling frustrated and irritated at not being able to get her alone as he had tried to do every day since the drama of the Nizam's visit.

Now there was that complacent look on his face which always annoyed her as he said:

"For once you cannot run away and you have to listen to me."

"I do not . . *have* to do . . anything, Mr. Blunt," Sita replied, "and I thought I had made it clear that I am not interested in anything you have to tell me."

"Are you not even interested that I have written half my poem to you which is so good that I feel future generations will read it when we are both forgotten."

"Then I hope future generations enjoy it."

She turned to the man on her other side hoping she could converse with him, only to find that he was a Muslim who spoke very little English and understood less.

After struggling for several minutes to start a conversation, Sita gave up the unequal task and tried to concentrate on her food.

"Will you be resting this afternoon?" Wilfrid Blunt asked in her ear.

"I expect so," Sita replied, thinking it would be one way of avoiding him.

There was however a smile on his lips that she did not like and it suddenly struck her that he might try to come to her room.

Her uncle was not in the Residency having left early in the morning for more consultations with the Nizam and his legal advisers.

It would be quite easy therefore for Mr. Blunt, if he wished to, to enter their Sitting-Room from the garden.

As if what she was thinking communicated itself to him he said softly:

"I have a great deal to say to you, but I promise I will not frighten you."

"You do not frighten me," Sita said untruthfully, "you merely make me feel angry and disgusted, and if you do what I think you are planning, I shall scream for the servants to turn you out."

Wilfrid Blunt laughed.

"You are certainly a formidable antagonist, Sita," he said. "But as I told you, I never give up the chase."

She did not reply and after a moment he said:

"I have been thinking it over while you have been so studiously avoiding me, and while it was a clever idea for you to invent someone with whom to be in love, I am convinced he is just a figment of your imagination, and does not really exist."

"Then you are mistaken," Sita said sharply.

"Nonsense," he replied. "I have been watching you very carefully since you have been here, and I am quite certain you are not in love either with Barnes, who is married already, or any of those unfledged *Aides-de-Camp*."

He gave a little laugh before he continued:

"That leaves only the Resident and myself as the recipients of your heart."

Sita wished she could tell him the truth, that she loved somebody who was brave and resourceful, and who had

132

saved her not only from dying, but from being still a prisoner in the Golconda Fort.

Then she told herself it was beneath her dignity to bandy words with Wilfrid Blunt.

Because he was so disliked by the Resident and his Staff she was quite certain that if she appealed to them for help in avoiding him they would be only too willing to tell him to behave himself.

Then she knew she would be unwilling to humiliate herself by admitting that she could not avoid this philanderer who was openly unfaithful to his wife, on whose money, she had learned, he depended for his very existence.

She did not miss the fact that he was extremely flirtatious with any attractive woman who came to the Residency as a guest at luncheon or dinner.

She had also overhead one of the other *Aides-de-Camp* say to Lieutenant Carstairs:

"I see our revolutionary poet is living up to his reputation. Did you see the way he was eyeing Lady Mallory last night?"

He was not aware that Sita was listening and Lieutenant Carstairs had replied:

"I was told of his many love affairs before he came here, so I am not really surprised at anything he does."

What she had overhead only confirmed what Sita already knew, and surprisingly it was Sir Harvey who told her when he was raging against something Wilfrid Blunt had said that he had at one time been associated with the most notorious woman in England.

"God knows what 'Skittles' saw in a chap like that!" he said scornfully. "But ever since then he has fancied himself as an irresistible 'Romeo'! Somebody should tell him to keep pursuing women and leave politics alone."

At the same time, it was obvious that Wilfrid Blunt had no intention of leaving her alone, and she thought now that if he did come to her room, she would have to struggle to prevent him from trying to kiss her again.

When luncheon was finished she went along the corridor which led to the Guest Wing, thinking if she did not rest she would have to find somewhere safe to read a book.

Then an idea came to her.

Like most of the guests in the Residency or Government House, she and her uncle had been allotted two bedrooms with a Sitting-Room in between them.

Sita therefore left the door of her own bedroom wide open and going into her uncle's room locked the door and shut the window which looked out onto the small verandah.

His other window was at the side of the building and it was impossible for anybody to enter through it without climbing over a flower-bed.

She lay down on the top of the bed, thinking that once again she had outwitted Wilfrid Blunt, and that was a satisfaction in itself.

At the same time, with every day that passed she grew more depressed and more apprehensive.

After the note she had received, she had not heard anything of the man she loved, nor had there been a communication of any sort from him.

She could not understand what had happened as she had been quite certain that now his mission was at an end, he would get in touch with her.

Instead there had just been silence.

Every night she sent her thoughts winging towards him through the darkness, and a dozen times a day she would look out into the sunshine and believe that her love was carried on the wind to wherever he might be.

But after the first happiness and elation of knowing he loved her and feeling the rapture and wonder of his kisses, she began to despair, thinking she might have lost him.

She did not really believe he no longer cared.

She was just afraid that something had happened, and he was either hurt or else by some miscarriage of justice had been taken to prison.

As the days passed she grew frantic, and she sought out Mr. Barnes to ask:

"What has . . happened about the . . Russian prisoner? You must forgive me for being curious . . but I cannot help . . wondering when he is being brought to trial."

There was silence, and she thought that Mr. Barnes looked embarrassed. Then after a moment, reluctantly, as if he felt he must tell the truth, he said:

"The man is dead. He was shot while trying to escape."

Even as he spoke Sita wondered if that was in fact the truth.

She thought it more likely that the Russian agitator had been disposed of, since a trial might have been too revealing as to how he had been captured.

Although he would have been executed anyway, it was more convenient that he should die without there being awkward revelations that were bound to react on those who had tracked him down.

This was all supposition on her part, but she was sure it was more or less the truth. Anyway, she was well aware that the laws of justice were very much more stringent when administered by the Nizam than by the British.

Because of what Mr. Barnes had told her she approached her uncle.

"Did you realise, Uncle Harvey," she asked, "that the agitator who was responsible for the attempt on the Nizam's life is dead?"

"Who told you that?" he asked sharply.

"I heard . . somebody say . . so."

"If he is, it is nothing to do with you, and the less you talk about it the better!"

"I am just wondering if he had a fair trial."

Sir Harvey looked at her suspiciously, then he said:

"You played your part in this very regrettable incident and got your reward for it. Now forget it! The Nizam is extremely popular and it is unlikely there will be any more attempts on his life."

Sita thought that was true. At the same time, what had happened to the man who had really saved him, and having knocked down his assailant had vanished into the crowd?

Because there had seemed to be almost a conspiracy amongst the Resident's staff not to talk about him, she became more and more certain that he was a member of '*The Great Game*' and therefore anonymous.

That brought her back to the question of how she would find him again.

"Come to me! Come to me! I want you!" she cried.

But because there was no answer, she felt as if her world was gradually returning to the darkness and despair she had known when she was in Wimbledon.

Locked safely in her uncle's room she thought she heard a sound in the Sitting-Room. Then as she listened, she heard a movement and realised that somebody was turning the handle of the door.

She knew who it was and held her breath. Then there were footsteps outside the closed window over which she had drawn the curtains.

The footsteps stopped and she knew that Wilfrid Blunt was standing outside on the verandah, perplexed by the closed and darkened window and wondering what he could do about it.

Then as if once more she had defeated him, she heard his footsteps walking away and gave a deep sigh of relief.

Only when she could hear him no longer, did she close her eyes and think only of the man who filled her thoughts to the exclusion of everything else.

* * *

The following morning was the fourth day since she had last seen him grappling on the ground with the Nizam's assailant, and the fifth since he had rescued her from the Golconda Fort, and she had been in his arms as they rode from there to the Barracks.

She thought as she lay remembering the ecstasy he had aroused in her at that moment that she had touched the glory of a Heaven she would never know again.

Now the darkness of despair was rising like a flood-tide to cover her.

136

'Perhaps he is dead,' she thought dully.

But she could not believe that he was without her knowing of it in her mind and in her heart.

"Trust me," he had said.

But for how long? And if he never returned, then all she would want would be to die, which he had forbidden her to do without his permission.

As if to confirm her fear that she had lost him for ever, her uncle said at breakfast:

"My work here with the Nizam is finished, and as I doubt if I shall have any further influence with the Viceroy, we may as well go home."

Sita stared at him incredulously.

"G.go home . . Uncle Harvey?"

"Yes," her uncle replied. "From all I have learnt, Lord Ripon is determined to go ahead with the Ilbert Bill, and I am just wasting my time."

"But . . Uncle Harvey," she objected, "you must stay until . . the Viceroy arrives here. The Durbar will take place in just over a week."

"What is the point of my staying here if he is not going to listen to me?" Sir Harvey asked disagreeably.

"I am sure he will, Uncle Harvey. After all, he consulted you when you were in Calcutta, and I am sure he will want to do so again."

Her uncle's lips were pressed together and she thought the reason why he did not wish to see the Viceroy or argue with him on the controversial Bill was that he thought it was a lost cause.

Whatever the feeling of the English in India, the Viceroy meant to go ahead with the Bill, and her uncle would perhaps be blamed for not having persuaded him to drop it.

"I will talk to the Resident today," he said rising from the breakfast-table, "and suggest we leave the day after tomorrow."

Sita gave a little cry that was almost that of an animal in pain.

As her uncle walked out of the room and shut the door

sharply behind him she knew it would be quite useless to plead with him even on her knees to stay longer.

And once she had left India her last hopes of finding happiness again would be doomed.

She wanted to cry, but was past tears, and she did not hear somebody come into the Sitting-Room until Lieutenant Carstairs said in an anxious voice:

"Are you all right, Miss Arran?"

With a superhuman effort Sita straightened herself in her chair, and managed in what sounded a more or less normal voice:

"Yes . . quite all right . . thank you, Mr. Carstairs. I just have a . . slight headache."

"It is not surprising," he said, "when you have been through so much."

He went to the breakfast-table, put down a piece of paper and went on:

"I have brought your uncle his programme for today, and here is one for you."

He smiled at her as he continued:

"I am afraid nothing very exciting is happening, except that there is a dinner-party, which is nothing unusual."

"I find them very . . interesting and . . enjoyable."

As Sita spoke she thought it would be the last dinner-party she would ever attend after she left for England.

Once they were back at Wimbledon she would be working again on her uncle's manuscript.

The only dinner-parties which would take place were when some old crony the same age as himself would be invited for a meal so that her uncle could pick his brains over something that had happened in the past.

On these occasions she was usually ignored while they ate, then told to make herself scarce when dinner was over.

Because she thought frantically that she must cling to everything that was Indian, not only because she enjoyed it so much but because it was in some way part of the man for whom she was yearning, she said:

"I am glad there is a party tonight. Will there be . . many guests?"

"Over thirty at least," Lieutenant Carstairs answered, "and the party is being given in honour of the new Governor of Bombay who was in the army. So you can expect a profusion of uniforms and a jingle of medals."

Sita laughed at the prospect.

"Then I shall wear my medal too," she said referring to the necklace given to her by the Nizam.

"I can hope I get one as good before I die!" Lieutenant Carstairs laughed.

"If it is as elaborate as mine, I do not know where you would wear it," Sita teased.

"If it is anything like as valuable," the Lieutenant replied, "I will wear it around my neck under my uniform where I could be quite certain it would not be stolen."

Sita managed to laugh, and when he had gone she thought that laughter was something else she would not hear again once she had returned to her uncle's house, and she would miss it.

She rose from the table to stand outside the open window on the verandah.

As she looked over the flower-filled garden towards the wide Musi River, she felt it would be impossible to go away and leave the beauty of India for the darkness of England.

Then as she looked at the river an idea came to her insidiously and temptingly.

She recognised it because it was the same idea and the same feeling she had had on the ship before she had left her cabin to seek the peace and rest of the sea.

But then he had come and prevented her from doing what he said was a wicked act, and she had promised him on her honour that never again would she attempt such a thing, unless he gave her permission to do so.

"But . . if you have forgotten . . if you no longer . . love me," she said to him in her heart, "why should it . . matter to . . you?"

139

She wondered if he was thinking of her contemptuously for her weakness, and she argued:

"It will mean that we will . . never be . . together, and perhaps in the next life I shall . . meet you more on . . equal terms. Then it will be . . easier."

She did not know quite what she meant by 'equal terms', except that she thought that perhaps at the last moment, after they had saved the Nizam's life, he had been too afraid to ask her to share his.

"Why did you not . . understand," she asked almost angrily, "that as I told you . . I would be happy in your arms . . whatever . . the conditions . . and however primitive . . our surroundings?"

She thought of the Khair-un-Nissa who had lived in the enclosed garden and had defied every principle on which she had been brought up to devote herself to an Englishman because she loved him.

Their love had surmounted a million difficulties of colour, religion and tradition.

Their happiness was still to be found vibrating in the place where whatever happened outside the garden, inside they were one complete person.

"That is what I want!" Sita cried aloud.

Because even to look at the beauty of the garden and the silver of the river hurt her she went inside.

Only when in the empty Sitting-Room did she find the tears were running down her cheeks and she could no longer control them.

*   *   *

The day passed slowly, and it was only when she had her bath before dinner that she remembered there was to be a party.

Because she felt that this was almost the last time she would be able to wear anything so elaborate and beautiful, she put on her white and silver gown with its big bustle and clasped her magnificent present from the Nizam round her neck.

As she waited for Sir Harvey to come from his bedroom

140

she felt as if there was a clock inside her head, ticking off the minutes until they should leave for England.

She knew that once tomorrow had passed, everything she did would be for the last time.

The words would repeat and repeat in her heart until she had to say goodbye to Hyderabad and leave for Calcutta where a ship would carry her back to England and her solitary life with her uncle.

"How can you do . . this to . . me?" she wanted to cry out aloud to the man who had deserted her.

Then a pride she had not until then realised she was capable of feeling made her lift her head high and walk down the long corridor which led to the Drawing-Room with a fixed smile on her lips.

Sir Harvey was more sullen than usual, and Sita thought it was because although he had decided to leave he was resentful and angry at the circumstances which forced him to do so.

They entered the Drawing-Room and as usual the guests were gathering there before the Resident appeared.

There was the chatter of voices and laughter which for Sita was part of India and something she would leave behind.

Lady Anne was wearing a gown of crimson silk that Sita had never seen before and she wore a tiara on her dark hair, as did most of the other women present.

Sita supposed it was in honour of the new Governor of Bombay who, like all the Governors, represented the Queen Empress.

After the Viceroy in importance came the Governors of Madras and Bombay, then the Lieutenant-Governors of the North-West Provinces and the Punjab and after them the Resident of Hyderabad.

Lieutenant Carstairs had been right in saying there would be a large number of officers in uniform present, and Sita thought how attractive they looked in their colourful mess dress.

'At least,' she thought to herself with a smile, 'they can wear the same uniforms every night, while the women are expected to ring the changes.'

She was aware that everybody who came to speak to her was admiring her necklace. While they exclaimed at the beauty of it, she was certain that they were actually thinking of its value.

Suddenly the buzz of conversation ceased.

The doors at the end of the Drawing-Room were flung open and the Resident appeared.

Tonight he was not alone. Beside him walked a man wearing the short red jacket of the Queen's Own Cameron Highlanders with its blue waist-coat, cuffs, and collar, his breast glittering with medals and decorations.

He was lithe and slim, and very much more impressive than the stout and red-faced Mr. Cordery.

Then as Sita looked at him casually she felt as if she had stopped breathing and it was almost impossible to move or think.

She could not believe what she saw, and told herself she must be dreaming.

As the Resident advanced into the room, introducing the man beside him to his guests, she knew it was he, the man for whom she had been waiting and praying and longing, until it had been an agony that was like a physical wound.

Now for the first time the stone which for the last three days had seemed to lie within her breast and had grown heavier and heavier hour by hour because she had been afraid she would never see him again, began to dissolve.

She felt as if she had been touched by a magic-wand and her whole being came alive.

She could feel the vibrations within herself reaching out towards him.

Then as he came nearer, shaking hands, and smiling politely to the people to whom he was introduced, she realised he looked different.

It was not only his clothes, it was that his hair was not

142

so black as it had been when she had last seen him, nor was his skin so dark.

In fact, now he appeared to have just the sunburn of a fair complexioned Englishman.

"How is it . . possible?" she asked herself.

Then as if in a dream she heard the Resident say:

"And now, My Lord, I want you to meet Sir Harvey Arran, a very distinguished Judge for many years in India, and who has come out of retirement especially to help the young Nizam with some very knotty problems that concern this Province."

"I am delighted to meet you, Sir Harvey."

It was his voice, and Sita drew in her breath.

It was the voice of the man who had said he loved her, the voice of the man who had asked her to trust him.

Then the Resident moved forward another pace.

"And now you must meet the heroine of the hour, whose swift action in stopping a would-be assailment saved the Nizam's life – Miss Arran – Lord Gale."

The man beside the Resident put out his hand towards her and for a moment Sita thought it was impossible to move, impossible, too, to meet his eyes.

Then almost without her being aware of it her hand was in his.

His clasp was strong and firm she knew without his saying so in words that he was loving her, and she belonged to him as she had from the moment he had saved her life, and made her his responsibility for ever.

*   *   *

Afterwards Sita could never remember what had happened at dinner.

She had had two distinguished soldiers on either side of her, who paid her compliments and admired her necklace, and she apparently answered their questions and made them laugh.

But she had no idea whether or not she ate anything during the long-drawn out meal.

All she was conscious of was the man seated at the

head of the table next to the Resident, and that just occasionally their eyes met.

Then it was as if their hearts flew across the intervening space between them and they were actually touching each other.

Only when it seemed to Sita as if a century had passed before the gentlemen came into the Drawing-Room to join the ladies after dinner did Lord Gale say to the Resident in a quiet voice:

"I wonder if it would be possible for me to have a word in private with Miss Arran? I have a message for her from the Viceroy, which I think should not be delayed, and actually I wish to add my own congratulations on her quickness in saving the Nizam's life. But I feel it would be embarrassing for her if I had to say it with such a large audience present."

For a moment Mr. Cordery looked surprised. Then he said:

"Of course! My private Sitting-Room is at your disposal My Lord. An *Aide-de-Camp* will show you and Miss Arran the way there."

Feeling that everybody was looking at her with curiosity but that it was unimportant, Sita moved to Lord Gale's side, and he offered her his arm.

As they left the Drawing-Room there was a burst of conversation and she was quite certain that the women, at any rate, were condemning what was happening, and at the same time, being extremely envious.

They walked in silence behind Lieutenant Carstairs, who was leading the way, and as he opened the door of the Resident's private room, he said:

"You will find a drink, My Lord, if you need one, on the table in the corner."

"Thank you," Lord Gale replied.

The door closed and as it did so he stood looking at Sita as if he would absorb every detail of her face, as she gazed at him with parted lips and an expression of such radiance in her eyes that it seemed as if a thousand lights had been lit inside her body.

Then when he did not speak, she asked:

"Why did . . you not . . tell me?"

The words were barely spoken before she moved forward into his arms and he held her close against him.

Then he was kissing her wildly, passionately, fiercely, as if he had been afraid of losing her, and now that he had found her was making her his.

He kissed her until the room swung dizzily around them, her feet were no longer on the ground, she was high in the sky, and the stars were once again in her breast and on her lips.

He kissed her until they were both breathless. Then as he raised his head he asked?"

"My darling, do you still love me?"

"I . . I thought I had . . lost you . . or else . . you had . . died," Sita whispered.

Then because of the agony through which she had passed her voice broke and tears came into her eyes.

"I came as swiftly as I could," he answered.

He was kissing her again and she could feel her heart beating frantically against his, and the stars on her lips became one with the fire she found on his.

"I love you! God, how I love you!" he cried. "My precious, I will make up to you for what I have made you suffer, but I swear there was nothing I could do about it."

"I . . understand," Sita said, "and I thought that . . you must be in '*The Great Game*' and that was . . why you were . . disguised."

"Is that all you thought?"

There were still tears in her eyes as she whispered:

"Because your . . disguise was so . . good I thought you must be an . . Eurasian, and that was why you had not . . returned to me after you . . saved the . . Nizam."

"*We* saved the Nizam," he corrected, "and in a way I am gratified that I deceived you so effectively. At the same time, my darling, it was very wonderful that believing what you did you were prepared to marry me."

"It would not have mattered to me what you were, or

how we had to live," Sita said. "In fact, I think I would have been happier if you had not been so important."

"Does it matter?"

She hid her face against his neck as she said:

"Suppose I . . fail you? Suppose I am not the . . right sort of . . wife that you should . . have as a . . Governor?"

He laughed, and it was a very tender sound.

"I cannot imagine anybody more suited to being a Governor's wife and, more important, my wife," he replied. "But, my darling, you may find it very dull and rather tedious after all the dramas in which you have been involved since the first moment I met you."

Sita blushed and pressed herself a little closer to him, knowing he was referring first to her attempted suicide, which he had prevented.

"I love you!" he said, his lips against her cheek, "and all we have to decide now, my lovely one, is how quickly we can be married."

Sita raised her head to say:

"Uncle Harvey has decided to go back to England the . . day after tomorrow. He is angry because . . the Viceroy will not . . listen to him."

"I will persuade your uncle to stay. At the same time, you are not going to stay with him. You are coming with me."

"It sounds . . wonderful but how . . how can I do . . that?"

There was a little note of passion in Sita's voice which he did not miss and he said looking down at her:

"How can you be so incredibly lovely and how have you dared to turn my whole life upside-down so that I find it impossible to think of anything except you?"

"As I have . . thought of you . . and been very . . very unhappy."

"I will make it up to you, I promise you that. But you must try to understand that I had to go back to Calcutta, and arrive formally from England, as I was expected to do."

"You mean . . .?" Sita asked.

146

"It is a long story and will take a long time to tell you in full, my beautiful," he said. "Briefly, I left India because my father had died and I had come into the title. When I saw Her Majesty the Queen she asked me to become the next Governor of Bombay, and I accepted. I then expected to put my father's affairs in order, and have a short rest before I returned to India."

"What . . happened?"

"I think you can very likely guess that I returned in a different capacity. I was asked to try to identify the man who was extremely dangerous to the peace of this country, and who was expected to board a P. & O. ship at either Alexandria or Port Said."

"So that was why you were travelling steerage?"

"Exactly!" he replied. "And as you are well aware, not under my own name."

"The name you . . refused to give me."

"I know," he said, "and it was very hard not to tell you that you could think of me and love me as Lenox Gale."

Sita gave a little laugh.

"Have I really at last got a name to call you, and to think about you, rather than . . just as 'he'?"

"I can think of more endearing names you could call me!"

His lips were very near to hers but she said:

"Please finish your . . story."

"I think you know the rest. I was almost sure the man was disguised as a Hindu, and mixing with the many other Hindus who were on board. He was part Russian, but there was a mixture of other nationalities in him. I suspected half-a-dozen other men before I finally found him."

"And then you . . found me!"

His arms tightened and he said:

"When I saw you walking along the deck I knew with an intuition which never fails me what you were about to do."

"And . . then?"

"When I had stopped you from doing anything so

147

wicked and so wrong, I knew you were the woman I had been looking for all my life."

"Oh! Darling! Is that really . . true?" she asked. "Did you fall . . in love with me . . at once?"

"I did not fall. My heart recognised you, then my mind told me I must never let you go."

"I am glad . . so very . . very glad that you . . saved me."

"So am I."

He kissed her until once again she knew an ecstasy that invaded her whole body, and sent thrill after thrill seeping through her.

Then as he released her he said:

"We cannot stay here too long. It will have them all talking. But, my darling, I am going to arrange that we are married here, so that you can come with me to Bombay. I cannot help thinking that the excitement our wedding will cause will outshine even the Viceroy's *Durbar*."

Sita gave a little cry of protest.

"Pl ..please . . could we not be married quietly? I should be . . shy and . . embarrassed otherwise."

"Even though that is what we would both prefer," Lord Gale said, "as I have already told you, news here flies on the wind, and there will be crowds outside as well as inside the Church. So we may as well do it properly. Besides, I am very, very proud of my bride!"

Sita knew he was right, and it would be a mistake for there to be anything secret about their marriage which might cause comment. Raising her face to his she said:

"As long as I can be your . . wife nothing else . . matters."

"Nothing!" he agreed.

He kissed her passionately and demandingly, until there was nothing more to say in words and they went back to the Drawing-Room.

As they entered they found, as was usual in India, that the guests who were not actually staying in the house had left immediately dinner was finished and there were only the Resident, his *Aides-de-Camp* and the house-party waiting for their return.

Lord Gale walked up to Mr. Cordery and said:

"I thought, Sir, that you would like to be the first to know that Miss Arran has promised to be my wife, and we would wish with your permission, to be married here in Hyderabad before I proceed to take over my new post in Bombay."

For a moment there was an astonished silence, during which even Sir Harvey was speechless.

Mr. Cordery recovered first and holding out his hand said:

"Congratulations, My Lord! You have certainly surprised me. I had no idea you even knew Miss Arran until this evening. But naturally I shall be delighted for her to be married from the Residency."

"Thank you," Lord Gale said quietly.

As the Resident gave her his good wishes for her future happiness and with unexpected gallantry kissed her hand, Sir Harvey came out of what was almost a trance to say:

"What is all this? Why was my permission not asked?"

"I am asking it now," Lord Gale replied, "and I cannot believe, Sir Harvey, that you would refuse not only to allow me to marry your niece, but also to stay in India and advise me for at least three months on the many knotty problems which I have already learned are waiting for me in Bombay."

If Sita had not been so busy admiring Lord Gale's tact, she would have laughed at the ludicrous expression on her uncle's face.

* * *

The next morning, after a night when Sita felt as if the angels were singing above her bed, and she was so rapturously happy that it was almost impossible to sleep, Lord Gale came to the Sitting-Room.

Her uncle had already left for what he said was the last of his meetings with the Nizam.

Because they were alone, Sita sprang up from the chair in which she was sitting to run into his outstretched arms.

Lord Gale kissed her until she was breathless, then he said:

"You are not to tempt me until we have been able to make our plans sensibly. When I look at you I can think of nothing but the softness of your lips and I just want to kiss you and go on kissing you."

"That is . . what I want," Sita said, "and I want . . nothing else for . . ever and ever!"

He smiled.

"I want a great deal more, but I will tell you about that when we are married. What is important is that the ceremony should take place as quickly as possible."

"I am ready to marry you now . . at this . . moment!" Sita asked passionately.

Then as his lips moved over the softness of her cheek she said:

"I suppose you realise that I have nothing to wear except the two beautiful gowns you have given me, and for which I have not yet thanked you?"

He did not speak and she went on:

"I wanted so much that you should see me in them, but perhaps it will seem a somewhat . . inadequate trousseau when I . . reach Bombay."

Lord Gale raised his head to look down at her and say:

"You are so ridiculously beautiful that I think the safest thing I can do is to make you dress like a Muslim woman, and enclose you in a secret garden like Khair-un-Nissa, and keep you all to myself."

"I would not mind," Sita replied, "but perhaps they would . . think it a little strange in . . these days . . on the part of an . . English Governor."

"I adore you!" Lord Gale said. "Actually you are going to work very hard as my wife, because there is a great deal for the Governor's wife to do. In fact the Viceroy was very relieved when I told him I was to be married."

"You were quite . . certain that I would . . accept you?"

"You already belonged to me for, as you pointed out,

I was responsible to you for the rest of my life. So I did not doubt that what I was saying was the truth."

"Of course it is the truth," Sita said, "and you know I love you . . and love you until all I can think of is that I shall be . . with you, and never again . . will I be so miserable as I was . . when you first saved me . . from the sea."

"I vowed then that I would look after you and protect you," he said, "and that is what I intend to do. I must also add that I will make you happy."

' "As I will try to . . make you."

"That is something that I am absolutely certain will be the most important thing in our marriage: a happiness which we have, I am convinced, learnt on the wheel of re-birth."

Sita gave a little cry of delight as she said:

"The next time we are re-born we shall be together, and from then on until all eternity! Could . . anything be more . . wonderful?"

"Nothing!" Lord Gale agreed.

He bent as if to kiss her and her lips were waiting for his, but then he set her on one side.

"Now listen," he said. "I have to tell you what I have arranged. We will be married tomorrow morning, and Mr. Barnes has already gone to make the arrangements in the English Church, which is not far from here. The Nizam has sent one of his staff to suggest that if it would please you, he will send us an elephant on which we can travel back from the Church to the Residency."

Sita stared at Lord Gale in surprise.

"How could the Nizam have heard so quickly that we are engaged?" she asked.

"I am quite certain that they knew it at the Palace long before we all went to bed last night," he smiled. "Anyway, that is his offer and, as I thought it would please you, I accepted."

"It will be something very, very different from the way any other English bride will travel!" Sita laughed.

"That is what I thought," he agreed, "and it will be

151

something to add to the stories of our adventures in India that we will be able to tell our children and our grandchildren.".

Sita blushed a little shyly, and he said:

"If you look at me like that, my darling, I shall find it impossible to tell you what else I have planned."

"Whatever it is, I know it will be perfect . . exciting and like a . . fairy-story."

"That is exactly what it is," he agreed, "and could it be anything else in this magical land that we both love and which had brought us together?"

Sita lifted her arms as if she would put them around his neck but determinedly he took both her wrists, and laid her hands in her lap.

"You are not to touch me," he said, "until I have finished what I have to tell you."

The look she gave him was mischievous, as she said:

"And suppose, Your Excellency, I disobey you?"

"Then I shall punish you," he answered, "by leaving you with only two gowns in your trousseau."

"That is a very awesome fate," she retorted, "but I doubt if even anyone as clever as you could provide me with many more by tomorrow morning."

"That is where you are mistaken," Lord Gale said. "The *Darzi* has been working very hard this past week and you will find you have a number of gowns, and one in particular which I think will be very suitable for your wedding."

"Do you . . mean it? Do you . . really mean it?"

"I mean it, my beautiful darling, because knowing how badly your uncle treated you with regard to your clothes I arranged for a dozen different materials to be made into gowns for you before I left for Calcutta."

He smiled at the astonishment in her eyes before he went on:

"They will be brought here late this afternoon so that they can be finished off together with several more, and the rest of your trousseau can be selected while we are honeymooning in a small Palace which the Nizam has offered to lend us in the Northern part of Hyderabad."

Sita gave a cry of delight.

"It is so wonderful that I am certain I am dreaming," she said, "and when I wake I shall find myself back at Wimbledon and everything, including you, will have vanished!"

"That is one thing that will never happen," Lord Gale said. "I shall not vanish, disappear or ever leave you, my darling. You are mine, and never again will you be lonely and frightened, or badly treated as you have been in the past."

He kissed her cheek and because she could find no words in which to thank him, she flung her arms around his neck and pressed her lips against his.

She felt the fire in his kiss and he held her so close against him that it was difficult to breathe.

"I love you, I want you!" he said. "Tomorrow night I shall be able to tell you how much you mean to me, and how we are united not only by our hearts, minds and souls, but also by our bodies."

The way he spoke made Sita feel shy, and yet something wild and wonderful within her responded to the passion in his words.

She pressed herself a little closer to him.

Then he pulled her to her feet and took her to the window so that they could look out over the Park.

For a moment he was silent. Then he said:

"I love you until my love fills the sky and touches the heights of Heaven. At the same time, my precious, you supplement my previous life which is India."

His voice was very tender as he went on:

"That is why it is so perfect because I think it will mean as much to you as it does to me. Therefore together we will work for the justice and the happiness of the people over whom we rule."

"You know that is what I want to do," Sita said, "and,

153

darling, anybody who is ruled over by you is a very . . lucky person."

He gave a little laugh that swept away the seriousness in which he had spoken. Then he said:

"What I have to do first is to teach you to trust me as I have a feeling that while you were waiting for my arrival you had begun to lose faith not only in me, but in your Karma."

"It was only because I . . loved you so much that I was . . afraid," Sita whispered.

"That is a very good way of excusing yourself," he replied. "At the same time, my precious, we should never doubt that the gods have blessed us, and because we have found each other our Karmas which started a million years ago have been joined today by our love."

Sita turned towards him to press her face against his shoulder and say:

"You say such wonderful things. You say all the things I want to hear, and I want to understand. Please, darling . . teach me to believe . . as you believe."

"I will teach you that, and also how to love me," Lord Gale said.

He put his fingers under her chin and turned her face up to his as he added:

"Teaching you about love, my lovely one, will not only be the most exciting thing I have ever done in my life, but also the most rewarding."

"Supposing I . . disappoint . . you?"

"You will not do that," he said, "and I think because, as I say, we have been moving towards each other for a million years, this is the moment when we reap the benefits of our experience apart to find perfection together."

He spoke so solemnly that Sita felt that to him such things were sacred, and because there were no other words in which to express her happiness, she again murmured against his lips:

"I love . . you! I love . . you! Please . . teach me to be . . exactly as you want . . me to be."

*   *   *

Sita looked at herself in the mirror and felt as if the happiness in her eyes lit the whole room.

It had been a long day of excitment and magic, a joy that she knew she would remember all her life.

For the moment she could only think that she was Lenox's wife, and that they were alone together and this was the beginning of their honeymoon.

They had been married in the British Church and in spite of her uncle's resentment, which he could not openly express, the Resident had given her away, and the Church had been crowded with every British personage of importance.

The Nizam and the Muslim leaders had come to the Reception after the ceremony, and to the crowd's delight the bride and bridegroom left the Church riding in a *howdah* on a State elephant.

Flowers were scattered all the way, and garlands flung onto the elephant's back until the gold and jewelled harness had been covered with them.

The gown that Lord Gale had chosen for Sita to wear had a huge bustle of white gauze embroidered with tiny pearls and diamonds so that she glittered with every move she made.

Somebody lent her, although she was not certain who it was until later, when she came to write the letter of thanks, a large diamond tiara to wear over her lace veil.

The Nizam had sent her as a wedding present a necklace of diamonds which was even more beautiful than the necklace he had given her already.

It made her feel like a Fairy Princess as she walked up the twenty-two white marble steps after she was married, and entered the Residency where the Durbar Hall was decorated with flowers.

It had taken nearly an hour for all the guests to file past them and congratulate them with a warmth and sincerity which Sita knew was not assumed.

She realised how important Lenox would be as Governor when they reached Bombay, and she had seen the

155

pomp surrounding the Viceroy in Calcutta which would also be his.

But here in Hyderabad she was the heroine because she had saved the Nizam's life, and although it was a little disappointing that she could not tell them that Lenox too had played a part in it, she was determined to enjoy her glory while it was hers.

They could not speak to each other as they drove to the railway station in an open carriage among a shower of flowers and cheers which made it impossible to hear anything they said.

"I wanted so much to tell them," Sita said to her husband when they could hear each other, "that you are a hero, not only in saving the Nizam's life, but also in many, many other of your exploits in 'The Great Game'."

She glanced at him as she spoke, knowing it was really something she should not say, and his voice was quite expressionless as he replied:

"I cannot imagine what you are talking about."

Sita laughed.

"If you are going to have secrets from me, then perhaps I will be sorry I married you."

"I will make you take that statement back tonight," he said. "Perhaps I may treat you as your uncle treated you!"

Now he was definitely teasing her, and she slipped her hand into his and said:

"I am no longer frightened and . . never will be again . . unless you say you . . no longer . . love me."

"That is an impossibility," he answered.

When they reached the station they found the State carriage which the Nizam had had attached to the train that was to carry them away was filled with flowers.

As soon as they left the station Sita melted into her husband's arms and he kissed her until there was nothing in the whole world but their love and their happiness.

It was a long journey and yet it seemed to pass like a flash.

The servants brought delicious food to their compartment at their first stop and waited on them, and when the train went on again they talked about themselves, and found there was so much to hear, so much to listen to, and so much to learn.

By the time they reached the exquisite little Palace which stood on the borders of a silver lake Sita knew she was even more in love than she had been before.

It was not until after dinner when again they talked over the past and looked forward to the future that she felt a little shy.

She loved him with every breath she drew, with every word she spoke, and yet she knew how inexperienced she was about love.

When she was undressed he came into her bedroom where the four-poster bed was draped with a mosquito net which seemed like a wedding-veil.

He set down his candle by the candle that was burning beside her, and lifting the net stood for a moment looking down at her as she lay back against the pillows with only a sheet covering her.

As she looked up at him a little anxiously, wondering what he was thinking, he said in his deep voice:

"Do you know how beautiful you are?"

"Is it . . really true that . . I am your wife?"

"You are mine! Mine, now and for ever!"

He got into bed beside her and put his arms around her so that her head was on his shoulder.

He felt her quivering against him, half with shyness, half with excitement, and thought it was the most thrilling experience he had ever known.

"Sometimes," he said, "when I was risking death and thought it would be impossible for me to escape detection I was afraid I might lose you."

"Oh, my darling, I am glad I did not know," Sita exclaimed. "I thought perhaps you were in danger and I was desperately afraid for you."

"Now it is all over."

"You have not . . told me what . . happens in . . the future."

"Whatever I have done, you know I cannot talk of it. That part of my life is a closed chapter."

"And now a . . new one . . begins."

"A very wonderful new one."

Gently he put her head back against the pillows so that he was looking down at her.

"First, my precious," he said, "I am going to spend a thousand and one nights teaching you about love."

"That is what I want," Sita interposed. "I love you and . . everything you do will be . . perfect and part of the stars which you . . gave me the . . first time you . . kissed me."

"I have no wish to frighten or shock you," he said quietly.

"You will never do that. To me, you are not only the most . . wonderful man in the world . . but also Krishna . . the God of Love . . and as the Indian women . . worship him . . I worship . . you."

He gave a little exclamation, as if he was deeply moved by what she had said.

"But you do realise," she went on, "that I am very . . ignorant and . . perhaps it . . will bore you."

"Do you think I want you to know anything but what I will teach you?" he asked. "I will kill any man who touches you."

The way he spoke made thrill after thrill run through her like shafts of moonlight.

He was everything, she thought, a man should be: strong, authoritative, commanding but at the same time tender and understanding.

"Love me," she pleaded, "and make me love you the way you . . want to be loved."

His lips held hers captive and he kissed her until she felt the fire on his lips light a flame within herself.

He pushed her nightgown away from her shoulders and kissed her neck and her breasts.

Then he was carrying her high into the sky, and she knew that they were experiencing the ecstasy of love which the gods in India brought to those who worshipped them.

It was the love that came from eternity and went to eternity and for which there was no end.

It was the love of life, the love that surmounts evil and suffering, and takes those who find it from the darkness into the light.

Other books by Barbara Cartland

Romantic Novels, over 300, the most recently published being:
The Vibrations of Love
Lies for Love
Love Rules
Moments of Love
Lucky in Love
The Poor Governess
Music from the Heart
Caught by Love
The King in Love
Winged Victory
The Call of the Highlands
Love and the Marquis
Kneel for Mercy
Riding to the Moon
Wish for Love
Mission to Monte Carlo
A Miracle in Music
A Marriage Made in Heaven
From Hate to Love
Light of the Gods
The Dream and the Glory
(in aid of the St. John Ambulance Brigade)

Autobiographical and Biographical
The Isthmus Years 1919–1939
The Years of Opportunity 1939–1945
I Search for Rainbows 1945–1976
We Danced All Night 1919–1929
Ronald Cartland (with a Foreword by Sir Winston Churchill)
Polly My Wonderful Mother
I Seek the Miraculous

Historical
Bewitching Women
The Outrageous Queen (The story of Queen Christina of Sweden)
The Scandalous Life of King Carol
The Private Life of Elizabeth, Empress of Austria
Josephine, Empress of France
Diane de Poitiers
Metternich – the Passionate Diplomat